THE DOOR-TO-DOOR BOOKSTORE

a novel

CARSTEN HENN

Translated by Melody Shaw

HANOVER
SQUARE
PRESS

If you purchased this book without a cover you should be aware that this book is stolen property. It was reported as "unsold and destroyed" to the publisher, and neither the author nor the publisher has received any payment for this "stripped book."

HANOVER
SQUARE
PRESS™

Recycling programs
for this product may
not exist in your area.

ISBN-13: 978-1-335-05009-0

The Door-to-Door Bookstore

Originally published in German as Der Buchspazierer in 2020 by Piper Verlag GmbH, Munich, Germany. This edition published in 2024.

Copyright © 2020 by Carsten Henn

English translation © 2023 by Melody Shaw

All rights reserved. No part of this book may be used or reproduced in any manner whatsoever without written permission.

Without limiting the author's and publisher's exclusive rights, any unauthorized use of this publication to train generative artificial intelligence (AI) technologies is expressly prohibited.

This is a work of fiction. Names, characters, places and incidents are either the product of the author's imagination or are used fictitiously. Any resemblance to actual persons, living or dead, businesses, companies, events or locales is entirely coincidental.

TM and ® are trademarks of Harlequin Enterprises ULC.

Hanover Square Press
22 Adelaide St. West, 41st Floor
Toronto, Ontario M5H 4E3, Canada
HanoverSqPress.com

Printed in U.S.A.

For booksellers everywhere:
in times of crisis they provide us with food for the soul.

"A novel is like a bow, and the violin that produces the sound is the reader's soul."

—Stendhal

chapter 1

A Man for All Seasons

IT HAS BEEN SAID that books find their own readers—but sometimes they need someone to show them the way. Living proof of this could be found at a bookshop in southern Germany, that went by the name of the City Gate. Admittedly, the name was an unusual choice, since the actual city gate—or at least what remained of it, which even locals often mistook for an avant-garde artwork—stood a good three streets away.

It was a very old bookshop, constructed and extended time and again over numerous historical periods. Extravagant architectural ornament and stucco rubbed shoulders with unadorned right angles. The glorious juxtaposition of the old and the new, the flamboyant and the restrained, which characterized the building's exterior also continued into its interior. Red plastic stands of CDs and DVDs stood next to frosted metal shelves of mangas; these in turn took their place next to globes displayed in polished glass cases, or elegant wooden shelves of books. Customers could find board games, stationery, tea, and even chocolate—a recent addition—for sale. The labyrinthine room was dominated by a heavy, dark counter known to employees simply as the Altar. It looked like a relic from the Baroque period: carvings on the front depicted a rural scene of a hunting party astride magnificent steeds, a pack of wiry dogs alongside, in pursuit of a group of wild boar.

Inside, one late summer's day, the question that is the raison d'être of every bookshop was being asked: "Can you recommend a good book?" The questioner, Ursel Schäfer, knew exactly what constituted a good book. Firstly, it must be gripping enough to keep her awake in bed reading until her eyes drooped shut. Secondly, it must contain at least three, preferably four, points at which she was moved to tears. Thirdly, it must have no less than three hundred pages, but no more than three hundred and eighty, and fourthly, the cover must never be green. Books with green covers were not to be trusted—bitter experience had taught her this on several occasions.

"Certainly," replied Sabine Gruber, who had been manager at the City Gate for the past three years. "What kinds of books do you enjoy reading?"

Ursel Schäfer did not wish to say. She wanted Sabine Gruber to know; after all, as a bookseller, she was surely naturally endowed with a certain level of clairvoyant skill.

"Give me three keywords, and I'll find just the right one to suit you. Romance? Rural? Cozy? Yes?"

"I wonder—is Mr. Kollhoff here?" asked Ursel Schäfer, her tone uneasy. "He always knows what I like. He knows what everyone likes."

"No, I'm afraid he's not here today. Mr. Kollhoff only works for us occasionally now."

"What a shame."

"Never mind, I have something for you. A family saga, set

in Cornwall. Look, the cover art shows the family's stately manor and grounds."

"It's green." Ursel Schäfer stared at Sabine Gruber in reproach. "Bright green!"

"That's because the story is set on the Earl of Durnborough's grand estate. It's had very good reviews!"

The heavy front door opened stiffly, setting the little copper bell above it tinkling brightly. Carl Kollhoff folded his umbrella, gave it his habitual shake, and placed it in the stand. His gaze scanned the bookshop he called home, on the lookout for new literary arrivals awaiting an introduction to his customers. He'd always likened himself to a beachcomber, who needed only a single glance to spy a hoard of treasures ready to be seized and freed from the grainy sand. As his gaze lit upon Ursel Schäfer, however, the treasures were forgotten in an instant. She threw him a warm smile, as though he were an amalgam of all the charming men she'd fallen in love with in the pages of the books he'd recommended over the years. In reality, Carl resembled none of those characters. He'd once had a small paunch, but over the years it had receded, much like the hair on his head, as though they'd entered into a pact to disappear together. Now, at age seventy-two, he was lean, but continued to wear his old, now-oversize clothes. His former boss, Sabine's father, had told him he'd begun to look as though his only source of nourishment was the words in his books, which were notoriously low in carbohydrates. "But rich in substance," Carl had always responded.

Carl wore rugged, heavy shoes of thick black leather with soles solid enough to last a lifetime. Good socks were also essential, in his opinion. These he combined with olive green overalls, and a matching collared jacket.

On his head, he wore a narrow-brimmed fisherman's hat, to protect his eyes from rain and bright sunshine. He never took it off, even indoors, other than to sleep. Somehow, he felt less than fully clothed without it. Nor was he ever seen without his glasses, the frames bought from an antique shop decades ago. Behind them peered shrewd eyes which bore signs of a lifetime of reading too long in poor light.

"Ms. Schäfer, how lovely to see you," he said, stepping toward Ursel Schäfer just as she took a step toward him, and away from Sabine Gruber. "May I recommend a book that would make ideal bedtime reading?"

"I so enjoyed the last one, especially when they gazed into each other's eyes at the end. A kiss would have been even better, to seal the deal, but on this occasion I'll settle for a gaze."

"It was almost more intense than a kiss, don't you think? Some gazes can be."

"Not when I'm doing the kissing!" For a moment, Ursel Schäfer felt deliciously wicked—a rare occurrence for her nowadays.

"This book," said Carl, taking one from the pile next to the till, "has been waiting for you since the moment it was unpacked. Set in Provence, and every word scented with lavender."

"Oh, Bordeaux-red books are the best! Does it end with a kiss?"

"Have I ever given an ending away?"

"No!" She pouted, but took the book from his hand.

Carl would never dream of recommending a novel without a happy end to her, but on no account would he rob Ursel Schäfer of the tiny thrill of wondering whether this one would be different.

"I'm so glad there are books in the world," she said. "I hope that's one thing that never changes! So many things do, and it happens so fast. Everyone pays with plastic money now. People give me such odd looks whenever I count out the right change at the till!"

"The written word will always remain, Ms. Schäfer; sometimes there is simply no better form of expression. Print is the best preserving agent for thoughts and stories; it keeps them fresh for centuries."

With a warm smile of farewell, Carl Kollhoff stepped through a door covered with advertising posters into a room that served as both stockroom and office for the bookshop. Inside was a desk barely visible under stacks of books and an old computer monitor framed with yellow Post-its. An enormous calendar covered in red pen dominated the wall.

As always, his book orders were waiting in a black plastic crate in the darkest corner of the room. In former times, their place had been on the desk, but since Sabine had taken the bookshop over from her father, the crate had migrated a little farther each day toward the least accessible corner. In tandem with its migration, the crate's contents had gradually reduced. Few people needed book delivery these days, and every year, their number continued to dwindle.

"Hiya, Mr. Kollhoff! What did you make of the game? That was never a penalty! The ref must've been blind!"

Leon, the new work experience lad, exited the tiny staff toilet, followed by a cloud of cigarette smoke. Anyone else would have known it was utterly useless asking Carl such a question. He never watched the news, never listened to the radio, never read a newspaper. He would have been the first to admit that he had lost touch with the world. It had been a deliberate decision, once all the reports of incompetent state leaders, ice cap melt, and suffering refugees had begun to sadden him more than the most tragic literary family saga ever could. It had been a form of self-preservation, even though his world had shrunk as a result. The world he now inhabited measured no more than two-by-two kilometers, and he patrolled its borders every day.

"Have you read J. L. Carr's fantastic book about football?" asked Carl, preferring to ask a question than to take sides on an issue of referee competence.

"Is it about our club?"

"No, it's about the Steeple Sinderby Wanderers."

"Never heard of them. Don't read books anyway. Only if I have to. In school. Even then, I try to watch the film instead." Leon grinned, as if this was a cunning way to make a fool of his teacher, rather than himself.

"Then why are you doing work experience here?"

"My sister did the same. Three years ago. We live around the corner—it's a short walk to get here."

Leon was to work at the bookshop for two weeks, as was customary for most students in Germany. He neglected to mention that anyone who failed to find a work experience place was forced to spend the allotted two weeks helping the caretaker, who would use the time, and a selection of suitably humiliating tasks, to take his revenge on the whole school body—as represented by the work experience students—for all the graffitied walls, old chewing gum stuck under desks, and discarded half-eaten packed lunches.

"Does your sister enjoy reading?"

"After she came here, sure. But that won't happen to me!"

Carl smiled. He knew exactly why Leon's sister had taken to reading. His former boss, Gustav Gruber, now a resident at the Münsterblick care home, had known exactly what to do with reluctant readers like Leon and his sister. He would set them to dusting each individual plastic-wrapped greeting card, one by one. The student in question was guaranteed— out of sheer despair at the tedium—to reach for the nearest book, which of course had been strategically deposited within easy reach by Gruber himself. Gustav Gruber had converted them all. He had always been good with children. To Carl, children had always been unfathomable creatures, even back when he himself had been one. And the further he left his own childhood behind, the more strange and peculiar they seemed to him.

Old Gruber had tempted Leon's sister with a novel in which a young woman falls in love with a vampire. For Leon, clearly brimming with raging hormones, Gruber would have left out a book with a beautiful teenage girl on the cover, and large-print pages. "It's important *that* they read, not *what* they read," old Gruber had always said. Carl couldn't quite endorse that view for all books: the ideas found between the covers of some were worse than poison, but more often than not, there was healing to be found on the page, sometimes even for ailments the reader hadn't realized they were suffering from.

With great care, Carl pulled the crate out from its corner. There were only three books lying forlornly inside. He took out brown paper and string to pack each book individually, as though it were a gift. Sabine Gruber had told him on numerous occasions he shouldn't bother, and to spare the expense, but Carl insisted. His customers would expect it. In a reflex action Carl was entirely unaware of, his hand stroked each cover before wrapping the books in the thick paper.

Finally, he picked up his olive green army backpack: marked with all the wear and tear of Bundeswehr use, but still in good condition thanks to Carl's care. Although it was empty, the fall of its cloth clearly indicated emptiness was not its natural form. He gently lowered the books between the heavy folds of the backpack, which he had lined with a soft blanket, as though he was carrying tiny puppies to their new owners. He arranged the three books in the backpack with the smallest resting farthest away, while the largest nestled next to his back, where it would not be compromised by the curve of the backpack.

As he was leaving, he paused, then turned to Leon. "Please would you dust the greeting cards? Ms. Gruber would like that. Best to bring them in here, then you can work in peace. I've always done it at the desk." Whisking Nick Hornby's *Fever Pitch* from the shelf where he'd spied it earlier, he laid it on the desk. The football pitch was a luscious shade of green—Ursel Schäfer wouldn't have given it a second glance.

Carl called it his round, although it resembled more of a polygon around the city center, without right angles or symmetry. The path traced by the ruins of the old city wall, standing like stumps of teeth in an old man's gums, was the boundary of his world. For thirty-four years, he had not set foot outside it; everything he needed in life lay within its borders.

Carl Kollhoff spent a lot of time walking, and he spent as much time thinking as he did walking. Only when he was walking could he think clearly; perhaps his footsteps on the cobbled streets were the one thing that could set his thoughts in motion.

A person walking at ground level might not notice it, but every pigeon and every sparrow knew the city was circular. Every old house and alleyway was oriented toward the minster, the cathedral which rose majestically in the center. If the city had been part of a model railway, you would say the minster had been built to the wrong scale. It dated from the short period in which the city had become very rich, a period that had come swiftly to an end before the minster could be completed, leaving one of the towers truncated still.

The houses stood reverentially around the minster; some of the older roofs even leaned at a deferential angle. They kept a respectful distance from the main entrance, allowing space for the largest and most beautiful square in the city: Münsterplatz.

As Carl stepped into the square, the feeling crept over him, as it had on previous occasions, that he was being watched, like a deer in a clearing, standing helplessly in the hunter's sights. He had to smile—in no other respect could he have been accused of resemblance to a deer. The aroma of the city was at its most intense in Münsterplatz. In the seventeenth century, the city had been besieged, and according to local legend, a baker had created the sugared wheel: a doughnut in the shape of a spoked wheel, filled with chocolate cream and sprinkled with powdered sugar. He took it to the besieging army, an edible message that they should leave. In reality, the calorie-dense confection had not been invented for a further two hundred years, a fact backed by documentary evidence, but the old story continued to thrive, and the city's visitors were eager to believe it.

Every day, Carl trod the exact same cobblestones of Münsterplatz in slow, even paces. If there was ever a person in the way, he would wait, increasing his stride afterward to regain the lost time. He had mapped out his route across the square so carefully that it could even be followed on market days. He had also ensured it traced a course that maximized his distance from the square's four bakeries, since he could no longer stomach the smell of the hot, greasy sugared wheels.

He turned into Beethovenstrasse, which in honesty was no more than an alley, not at all worthy of the great composer. An entire district had been named after famous composers, courtesy of an employee at the planning office who had wanted to make his own mark. The widest street had been reserved for Schubert, the employee's personal favorite.

Although Carl Kollhoff was not aware of it, he stood at that moment at the exact center of his world. It was bordered on two sides by tram lines, the 18 and the 57. (In fact, the city only had seven tram routes, but it had been felt that higher numbers would add a nice metropolitan air, at least to its public transportation.) On another side was the fast road from the north, and on the fourth was the river, which for most of the year was content to burble picturesquely, and only surged to high water for a few days in the spring, rising to emit a modest roar, like a lion cub with underdeveloped vocal cords.

His first call of the day took him into a lane by the name of Salierigasse, to the home of Christian von Hohenesch. A pedestrian hurrying by would not have noticed the dark stone villa's grandeur: it stood a step back from the other buildings, crouching like a hunched black swan waiting for its moment to spread magnificent wings. Behind it lay gardens bordered by a square of gigantic oak trees, with three benches positioned to enable Christian von Hohenesch to read with the sun falling on his book at any time of day.

Carl was aware that Hohenesch possessed enormous wealth, but not that he was the richest man in the city. No one knew, least of all Hohenesch himself, who never compared himself with others. His family had made their fortune generations ago in the tanning trade by the river, and succeeded in not losing it again during the industrial revolution. Christian von Hohenesch had no need to work; he allowed his shares and investments to work for him. He simply managed his wealth managers. A housekeeper came once a day to cook and clean the few occupied rooms; a gardener came once a week to trim the hedges and maintain the sun's passage to his books; a caretaker service visited once a month; and from Monday to Friday, Carl came with a new book, which Christian von Hohenesch had usually finished reading by the following day. As far as Carl knew, Hohenesch had not stepped beyond the borders of his kingdom in an eternity.

Carl pulled on the copper rod by the door, and a bell rang a low note in the villa's interior. As usual, there was a pause while the householder walked the long, dark corridor; then the heavy door creaked open, just a crack. Christian von Hohenesch never stepped outside. He was a handsome man: tall, dark-haired, with sculpted cheekbones, a striking chin, and a sadness that settled over his features like fine gray dust. As always, he wore a dark blue double-breasted suit with a fresh white orchid in the buttonhole, and his black leather shoes shone as if he was dressed for the Opera Ball. Hohenesch was much younger than his clothing suggested: barely thirty-seven years old—but he had worn suits since early childhood, and they felt as natural to him as jeans did to others.

"Mr. Kollhoff, you're late. We had agreed a quarter past seven," said Hohenesch by way of greeting.

Carl bowed his head in acknowledgment, then carefully reached for his backpack. "I've brought your new book." He straightened the string's bow, which had shifted on the journey.

"I hope it lives up to your recommendation." Hohenesch took the book, but did not unwrap it. It was a novel about Alexander the Great, set during his time under Aristotle's instruction. Hohenesch read only philosophical works.

He handed Carl a tip, calculated according to the book's weight, which he had researched in advance. "Please be punctual again next time. Punctuality is the politeness of kings."

"Of course. Enjoy your evening."

"Yes, I hope yours is equally pleasant, naturally."

Christian von Hohenesch closed the solid wooden door, and the villa once more appeared deserted.

The master of the house would have loved to discuss books and authors in depth with Carl, whom he regarded as an educated, well-mannered man, and a kindred spirit. But with the passage of time, the words of invitation had escaped him. Perhaps he had lost them among the many rooms in his grand home.

★ ★ ★

Carl took his leave of Christian von Hohenesch—yet in his mind, it was another person altogether he left behind. Everywhere in the real world, Carl saw reflections of novels. To him, the city was populated with characters from books, even if those characters lived in quite different times, or far-off lands. To Carl, the moment Christian von Hohenesch had first opened the heavy door of his villa, he had stepped out from the pages of *Pride and Prejudice*. Carl was now bidding farewell to Pemberley in eighteenth-century Derbyshire, and to its owner, Fitzwilliam Darcy, who, despite his impeccable manners, could at times appear harsh and arrogant.

Carl's inability to remember any name, unless it belonged to a book character, had begun during his school days, when so many of his classmates had given their teachers nicknames, most of them unflattering: Loobrush, Prince Morphine, or Spitty. Carl had given them different names: Odysseus, Tristan, or Gulliver. Unlike his classmates, when he graduated high school with his Abitur qualification and the offer of an apprenticeship at the bookshop, his habit of assigning nicknames had persisted. The young lad slouching along in a threadbare uniform every day as Carl made his way to the bookshop became the Good Soldier Schwejk. The greengrocer who sold him apples transformed into the wicked queen from *Snow White*—mercifully, she refrained from poisoning her fruit. At some point, Carl had realized that his city was full of literary figures; every inhabitant had their literary counterpart. In the years that followed, he met Sherlock Holmes, head of the murder squad in the city police; he even met Lady Chatterley, who often opened her door wearing a flimsy robe, and for whom he developed a slight crush as a young man. Sadly, she left the city with Adso of Melk. Captain Ahab obsessed over an enormous mole which wreaked havoc in his garden, and which he consistently failed to hunt down. Carl delivered books about South America to Walter Faber, a chronically ill engineer, right up until his death. And in an apartment building that had once been a prison, the Count of Monte Cristo lived behind barred windows, a feature which the new owners had on a whim decided to retain.

He found that a suitable literary name always occurred to him long before he succeeded in memorizing the real one. It was as though his memory wished to prevent him from burdening it with anything so profane. From the moment he selected a name, he ceased to see the real one. On their way from his retina to his brain, the letters of *Christian von Hohenesch* would be miraculously transposed into *Mr. Darcy*, entirely without Carl's awareness. Only in very particular situations would his mind relent and provide a real name—and these days there were precious few it needed to recall.

Carl's route through the winding alleyways next took him to a literary figure with a fate far bleaker than that of the Pemberley gentleman whose story concluded with a happy marriage.

His client was waiting behind the door, peering through the spyhole at the few passersby in the street beyond. No one came here for a stroll. No one came to admire the buildings; the handsome architecture stopped several streets away. In this part of the old city, pedestrians increased their pace, as though they could not bear the oppressive narrowness of the street, with its gables looming overhead, threatening to close ranks and block out the daylight.

The slender young woman behind the spyhole knew at what time Carl would arrive. She also knew that it was foolish to spend long minutes peering through the door, instead of waiting in the living room for the doorbell, but she was unable to tear herself away. Andrea Cremmen brushed a lock of blond hair behind her ear and tugged her dress straight. From the time she started kindergarten she had always been the prettiest girl in the room, a quality which had earned her both affection and envy—and an early marriage to Matthias, a man with a promising career in the insurance industry, who worked long hours in the evening and on weekends to give them a comfortable life. Andrea herself was a trained nurse, but now worked half days at a small doctor's surgery, where she had been put behind the reception desk, because the sight of her calmed and lightened the spirits of the patients. No one had needed to tell Andrea to smile; she did so quite naturally—it was part and parcel of being pretty. A pretty person who doesn't smile looks arrogant, so she smiled all day.

She had never dared to look anything other than perfect. What would happen then? What would others see in her? But Carl Kollhoff seemed like a man to whom she could show her unsmiling face. He would find the right words to describe what appeared there. Andrea knew that he chose his words as carefully as a perfumier selecting ingredients for an expensive scent. She let her smile drop, and pulled the lock of hair forward, permitting herself a few strands of disarray.

Spotting Carl in the street, she tucked the strands swiftly back behind her ear again.

Carl rang the bell, and waited. He knew Andrea Cremmen always took a little time to open the door, and was always slightly breathless—but she always wore a smile of pleasure.

A key rattled in the lock, then the door opened.

"Mr. Kollhoff, you're early today! I hadn't expected you yet. I must look in a terrible state." She ran her fingers through her glossy hair, styled to perfectly complement her elegant dress in a red rose print.

Carl found her bewitching, and yet the sight of her always made him feel a little sad too. Behind all her beauty lay something he could not quite put a finger on—but it had something to do with the package he now handed to her: one of the books Andrea Cremmen loved so well. The book's weight was perfectly acceptable (Carl liked books to have the appropriate weight: heavier than a bar of chocolate, lighter than a liter of milk); it was the weight of the contents that gave Carl concern.

"Is it a good one?" she asked, pulling the string on the packing paper straight.

"From what I've heard, *The Shadow Rose* lives up to the author's other works."

"Highly dramatic?"

Now it was Carl's turn to smile. There was an unspoken agreement between them: when he brought her a book, it was always dramatic, with a tragic end. In the past, he had occasionally recommended books with a happy end, but she had never enjoyed them. She found they bore no relation to reality. Andrea Cremmen loved novels in which the female protagonist suffered and either died or was left unhappy and alone at the end. Open endings were only acceptable if they held out the possibility of one or the other.

"As always, I retain my right to silence," said Carl. "How did you like the last novel?"

Andrea Cremmen took a deep breath and shook her head. "It was so sad! She walks into the water at the end... Why didn't you warn me?" She gave a playful pout.

"I can't possibly do that."

In the past he had packed her books in bright, cheerful gift wrap, but after a while that had felt disingenuous.

"Will you bring me another next week? I've heard about a novel where it's night all the time—it takes place in Greenland in the winter. And the main character has lost her child. Do you know it? I thought it sounded good."

Carl had heard of the book. He'd hoped Andrea Cremmen hadn't.

"I'll bring it." Carl didn't say he'd bring it gladly, because that would have been untrue.

"Can you interest me in anything else?"

"There's a crime story set right here in this city; it's only just been published. I've not read it yet, but I hear it's very funny."

Andrea Cremmen waved the suggestion aside. "Do you think I'd enjoy it?"

Carl made a point of never lying. Send a lie out into the world, and you can never retrieve it. "No."

"I don't think so either."

"But it might make you laugh. And you have a beautiful laugh—I hope that's not too forward of me. I'm sure you've heard what Charlie Chaplin said, 'A day without laughter is a day wasted.' We have so few days on this earth, we can't afford to lose any." He'd never said anything like this to her before. Perhaps he'd sensed her unhappiness was greater than usual today? Carl didn't know. Sometimes his mouth just went ahead and said things without consulting his head.

Andrea Cremmen was no longer smiling. Her lower lip trembled slightly. "You've saved my day, thank you!" The door closed abruptly.

Carl watched the door close, not on Andrea Cremmen but on Effi Briest: a sorrowful young woman, married too young, whose sad fate was every bit as tragic as that of the numerous heroines in the books Andrea Cremmen ordered. Carl wished he could do more for her than deliver books that proved others can suffer too, but without any guidance on how to end the suffering.

Behind the door, Andrea Cremmen suppressed her tears. She longed to tell him what had happened that day, but that would have entailed reliving it, which was more than she could face. She unwrapped the package with trembling hands and had begun reading the book before she left the hallway. One of the characters had taken their own life by the end of page one.

Carl had taken no more than a few steps when he heard a soft mew beside him. Looking down, he saw a gaunt, three-legged cat looking up at him, its fur scruffy, its ears notched from numerous battles. Carl had no idea whether it was male or female, or where its home was, if indeed it had one. But they were good friends, nonetheless. While others had house cats, Carl had a street cat.

"Hello, Dog," he said and smiled. He'd given the cat this name because it behaved like one: sniffing at everything as it walked, and marking its territory. Dog never purred; it growled. When Carl arrived at a customer's door, Dog never sat—it lay down. It could lie down anywhere, even on the narrowest of steps.

Dog pressed itself against Carl's leg, then ran ahead, turning with a look of impatience. The animal was intelligent enough to guess there would be something to eat at Carl's third delivery of the day. Four streets away, near the Elisenbrunnen fountain, lived an old woman who was the exact opposite of Effi Briest: high-spirited, cheerful, and always dressed in colorful clothing. More often than not, he would find her wearing mismatched socks or shoes, or with one strap of her overalls hanging down over her shoulder. Her apartment was full of belongings stacked like mountains, with narrow paths like valleys running between. The old woman reminded Carl of a character in a children's story: a wild young girl who shaped her world as she pleased. This older version of the girl, however, never set foot into the real world; she was afraid of open sky.

A little over seven years ago, she had just spent a beautiful summer's day with her husband in their garden, sitting in the shade of a walnut tree, when a storm had blown in, with rain and wind, but most of all with violent force. They had already returned to the house when they realized they had left their bins on the street—an act of negligence guaranteed to cause complaint among the neighbors. Her husband had gone out in the storm, despite her attempts to prevent him. *It won't take a minute*, he'd said. *I'll be right back.* At exactly that moment, a tile had come loose from their own roof, and had been rapidly transformed by the wind into a missile his head could not withstand.

Since then, she hadn't cared what the neighbors thought. And since then, she had never stepped out of doors.

When she opened the door, she would never say "Good evening, Mr. Kollhoff," "Hello," or "How lovely to see you." Instead, she would greet him with "Wooldouse," "He was a used cat dealer," or "Glass roots." Today, when he rang the bell, she exclaimed "Frogiveness."

It was then Carl's task to invent a plausible impromptu definition.

"*Frogiveness*, derived from *frog-I've-ness*, denotes the path toward recognizing the innermost core of the self. The concept references the fairy tale *The Frog Prince*, which appears as the first tale in *Grimms' Fairy Tales*. Behind the concept of frogiveness lies the hypothesis that each person has an inner frog which they must transform with love—a kiss, in the fairy tale—into a handsome prince. The theory first appears in literature in 1923 in Sigmund Freud's work *The Id, the Frog, and the SuperFrog*."

Mrs. Longstocking offered him a cherry bonbon by way of reward. A less apt definition would have received a lemon bonbon. In return, he handed her the book she had ordered. As always, he had drawn a large red rose on her packing paper. Mrs. Longstocking read everything, from classic adventure stories to science fiction to humor: anything, provided the content was light—nothing that could drag her back into the depths of reality.

"The day after tomorrow, I'll have another word for you," she said. "It's a particularly hard nut to crack." Bending down to Dog, she offered something from her pocket. It was swallowed in one gulp before she even had time to close the door.

Although Carl's backpack was now empty, he had one more call to make. Every visit to this next client was a pleasure: he had the warmest baritone voice Carl had ever heard. If a sofa could be covered with the sound of a voice, only this man's would do. To Carl Kollhoff, he was from Bernhard Schlink's *The Reader*: the young Michael Berg, who falls in love with a woman twenty years his senior and begins to regularly read aloud to her. In the case of Carl's client, the audience were the workers at a cigar factory which had been built a few years earlier, the only one in the region. The management had provided a budget for someone to read aloud from books through the working day, as was the practice in Cuba. The whole thing was predominantly a marketing stunt, and the Reader earned very little from it, but he was so devoted to his work that he constantly wore a scarf around his neck to warm his vocal cords. To protect his voice, he rarely spoke outside the cigar factory, so Carl had been more than a little surprised to receive a private phone call asking him to deliver not a book, but a brand of throat pastilles only available from the pharmacy next to the bookshop. The Reader did not wish to venture out onto the streets, where a wave of flu was currently sweeping the city. Out of the same precaution, his door opened by the smallest possible crack to receive the package, and give Carl both a grateful smile and the payment, together with generous tip (which Carl would have preferred to refuse, since he knew how little the Reader earned). The Reader took a pastille from the tin, and swiftly closed the door to his rented apartment within a housing block that was so austere, the builders had clearly spared all expense on anything that might give the exterior any sense of beauty or love. It was as utilitarian as a cage for battery hens.

Carl always felt sad when his backpack was empty: all that was left now was the homeward stretch. Not that he disliked his home, but Dog never followed him there, and there was no other living thing waiting behind the door of his apartment to press against his legs and look expectantly at him when it wanted to be stroked. The final leg of his round took him through the city cemetery. It was over two hundred years old, with a large statue of the grim reaper at its center, a knowing smile carved into the face of its bony skull. Somehow, the familiarity with the eventual destination of his life's path took away the fear for Carl, and he found the cemetery's beauty calming.

The plate next to Carl's doorbell read E. T. A. Kollhoff. This was not entirely untrue, since the surname was correct. Carl had always admired the author E. T. A. Hoffmann, on account of his initials. How many people had three, aside from J. R. R. Tolkien, or C. P. E. Bach? Three initials signified something special; a great deal could be concealed behind three. They had the air of holding a great secret, such as why their owner did not fully write out any of the names.

Occasionally, letters would be returned, if a new postman failed to identify Carl as the man behind those initials. He saw no reason to alter the nameplate. At seventy-two years old, he no longer received much post in any case. The post he did receive was never grounds for joy, so it was welcome to take another turn in the sorting office.

Carl's apartment had too many rooms. Four in all, plus a

small kitchen, a windowless room with a bath, and another with a toilet. Sometimes he looked on them like flower beds in which nothing had grown. Two of the rooms had been intended for his children: one would have been a room for a girl, with its window to the green inner courtyard; the other for his son, looking out over the street, where he could watch the cars going by. But Carl had never found his very own Mrs. Kollhoff, so never had children. He had kept the apartment regardless. In all the decades, the rent had never been increased; it had probably been forgotten.

Now he lived with his paper family, kept in cabinets behind frosted glass doors to protect them from light and dust: books needing to be read over and over, just like pearls that need to be worn to make them more beautiful, or animals needing to be stroked to feel loved. Sometimes it seemed to Carl that each word was a cell of his own body; it was at that point he knew that with the years of reading he had absorbed them into himself.

Carl understood people who collected books like others collected stamps: people who loved to let their gaze wander along book spines, who gathered books around themselves like a community of close friends. Inside books lived the characters to whom they felt a connection, with destinies unfolding in which they shared, or wished they could.

Carl hung his green jacket on the hook behind the door, with his backpack alongside, and pulled them straight. Then he went into the little kitchen to sit at the Formica table with a slice of black bread spread with butter and salt, a glass of sauerkraut juice, and a green apple, quartered.

The apartment had been advertised as "with balcony." This consisted of a cast-iron balustrade in front of the French windows beside which his old armchair sat. On the chair lay a book with a till receipt tucked inside as a bookmark. From this vantage point, he could watch the old city, keeping a lookout for any of his clients passing by, or Dog leaping across the rooftops—which it never yet had. Carl always read until ten on the dot, then washed and went to bed. As the cover settled over him, he felt wrapped in the comforting assurance that the next day would bring a new selection of very special books to deliver to his very special clients.

chapter 2

The Stranger

YET AGAIN, Carl woke feeling like a book with missing pages. The sensation had been growing over the past few months, and it crossed his mind that perhaps there was not much paper left between the covers of his life story.

He brewed coffee in the kitchen. Warmth spread through his sleep-cold fingers wrapped around the porcelain of the cup. A sliver of cheer accompanied the warmth, slowly expanding and spreading little by little through his body like a gentle wave. He only ever used fine porcelain cups, even though they were more expensive and broke more easily; he couldn't feel anything through the thick sides of a mug.

The day rushed by like a grainy black-and-white film populated with shadowy figures performing dimly recognizable actions. Only when the bell above the door of the bookshop announced Carl Kollhoff's arrival at six thirty did color flood into his life.

Sabine Gruber stood behind the counter like a soldier at a

barricade, deliberately stationed on a spot that would prevent any customer from seeing the gold-framed newspaper article on the wall behind her. Accompanied by a half-page photo, it was a piece on Carl's unusual book delivery service. There had even been a TV program. After its broadcast, a lot of people started ordering books for personal delivery. The novelty had soon worn off when the customers had realized that, at heart, they were TV viewers, not book readers.

There were two books in Carl's crate today. Slim volumes, yet they felt heavy to Carl as he strapped them into his backpack.

Leon was squatting on the carpet next to the stand of undusted greeting cards, staring fixedly at his phone. *Fever Pitch* lay unopened on the table: Nick Hornby's words were clearly struggling to be heard above the clamor of voices on the world wide web.

"Off on the beat again?" asked Leon, without looking up from the screen.

"I'm not a police officer," replied Carl. "I deliver books. The only crime I'm likely to discover would be their contents."

"Don't you get bored?" Leon still didn't look up. Carl had the distinct impression the lad wasn't interested in an answer, but when asked a question, Carl always replied with a response as honest as it was appropriate.

"I'm like a clock hand. You might think the hand is unhappy, always covering the same ground, always returning to where it started, but the opposite is true. It appreciates the certainty of its path and destination, the security that it cannot go in the wrong direction, that it will always be useful and precise." Carl stared at Leon, who still did not return his gaze.

"Okay, I get it," he said.

Pulling his jacket collar straight, Carl stepped outside with a feeling of warmth at the task ahead. He could not know that today, a different task would arise: a task much weightier than a bulging backpack.

It was the kind of autumn day that still dreamed of summer. Münsterplatz was bathed in evening sunlight, its old walls looking young again, the old city gleaming like a new build.

The moment Carl Kollhoff's feet touched the cobblestones, polished smooth by innumerable leather soles worn by countless generations of feet, the feeling of being watched stole over him again. It was so strong, he stopped and looked around, turning on the spot like a lamp in a lighthouse. People sailed past him—some racing by like speedboats, others drifting like rafts—but none of them paid him any attention.

He could feel the urgency in his legs as they twitched in time to the passing seconds, impatient to keep to schedule. He resumed walking, trying to swat the feeling away like a troublesome fly, but it would not be shaken off.

Suddenly, a little girl with dark curly hair was walking next to Carl, matching her stride to his.

She looked exactly like the main character in *A Castle for the Princess*, a picture book with a pocket full of doll clothes inside the back cover, which readers could attach to pages where the princess appeared. She also bore a resemblance to the heroine of *Lily and the Friendly Crocodile*, who helped a crocodile fight the villainous Kaspar. Admittedly, you would have to imagine these literary heroines dressed in a vibrant yellow winter coat with fat wooden buttons, accessorized with yellow knitted tights and light brown sheepskin-topped boots. But undoubtedly the most striking aspect of this small person was the leather helmet with attached goggles: clearly a fashion accessory, rather than evidence of any competence at piloting propeller-driven aircraft. Imagine the pollen grains blown from a sunflower into the child's face, and coming to rest as freckles. They had congregated around her snub nose as though it was the most beautiful part of her entire face. Her eyes were a pale blue, more sky than sea.

"Hi, I'm Schascha. I'm nine years old." The way she spoke contained no demand that Carl reciprocate with his own name and age. It was information, not an invitation. She was small for her age, which was the cause of no small amount of teasing in school. She also believed she was a bit too fat, although this was in fact nothing more than the reserves a young body lays down in preparation for a growth spurt.

Carl's pace did not slow: the books had to reach their readers with all speed. They may not have been soft fruit, but he still regarded them as perishable goods.

"Aren't you scared of me?"

"Nope."

"I'm sure you're not allowed to go with strangers."

"You're not a stranger. I know you."

"No, you don't."

"I watch you walking across Münsterplatz every day. From my window. Have done ever since I could think. And I started thinking very early in life, so my dad says. And I haven't stopped since. You've been there the whole time. Like the sound of the bells ringing from the minster. So, I do know you." The words bubbled out of her like a fountain.

"If you know me, what's my name?"

"I don't know the names of the minster bells either, but I'd recognize them anywhere, even if a hundred thousand million others were ringing together. The same as I can spot you out of a crowd of other people."

Carl was not convinced by this line of argument. It struck him as too childlike. "In that case, you don't really know me, so I'm a stranger."

"You're the Book Walker. That's what I call you. There, you have a name, and I know it."

Carl sighed. "If you've been watching me for that long, you must know I always walk alone."

"That's fine. You walk alone, and I'll walk alone beside you."

"No," said Carl, "that's not possible."

Although he liked children, he did not understand them in the slightest. His own childhood lay so far in the past that the memories were as faded as old Polaroids. And while he got older every year, children remained children, widening the distance between them as the years went by. He was no longer sure it was a gap he could bridge.

He walked on, leaving Schascha behind.

The following day, Schascha was there again. At first she said nothing, simply walking beside him and observing him. "I thought carefully last night about whether you could be dangerous. Because you asked whether I was scared of you." She pointed to his feet. "You don't have a dangerous walk."

Carl looked at his feet and watched the way they stepped. He had never thought about whether they moved in a dangerous fashion. But he had spent the previous evening considering what he would do if Schascha reappeared. The answer had been that on no account would he take her on his round. "Maybe I have a dangerous walk when I've turned the corner into the narrow streets of the old city?"

"I don't think so." She shook her head, and the dark curls shook along with it.

"I might be a child snatcher!"

"No, you aren't." Schascha wasn't at all impressed.

"Shall I prove it?"

"You're too slow."

"Are you sure? Shall I catch you?"

"Seriously?" Her chin drew in, and her eyebrows rose in a skeptical arch.

"I'll do it!"

"Go on then. Or are you still thinking about it?"

Carl was circling Schascha, who continued to stare at him. He waited until she blinked, then lunged forward. She dodged easily. It was a small step to one side, nothing more. He lunged again, and again she stepped effortlessly aside, laughing all the while.

"We play catch at school all the time! I'm the second best. Only Svenja's better than me, but she's better at everything, so it doesn't count. She's really mean too—she gives us all a mark for how good a friend we are, and she's always changing it."

Carl refrained from any further attempts to catch Schascha. He'd already made enough of a fool of himself. He hoped no one had seen him; after all, he had a reputation to maintain.

Schascha grinned at him.

"You're not afraid of me, but it sounds like you're afraid of Svenja."

She nodded. "Totally. But everyone is. Better to be afraid of her. You'd be afraid of her too."

Carl barked a laugh. It felt like an old, rusty engine suddenly springing to life.

"You've got a funny laugh," said Schascha, "like you don't quite know how."

"Everyone knows how to laugh."

"Not my aunt Bärbel, she never laughs. No one laughs where she comes from."

"So where does she come from?"

"Sweden, I think."

"And why don't people in Sweden laugh?"

"Because it's so cold there in the winter. If you open your mouth to laugh, the cold air gets in around your teeth, and that hurts super bad. So they only smile. Aunt Bärbel waves her hands about when something's funny, or sometimes she stamps her feet up and down."

Carl turned into Salierigasse. "Your parents must be worried where you've got to."

"My dad's still at work, and my mom's dead."

Carl stopped, and gazed into Schascha's blue eyes. "I'm sorry to hear that."

"Which?"

Carl reflected for a moment. "Both. But much more so the second."

"Mom's just a photo on the hall table. I don't remember her, so I don't think I can be sad that she's dead." Smiling, she pointed to her mouth. "Dad says I've got Mom's laugh, and her smile. That's why I laugh a lot. It feels like my mom's laughing with me. Does your mom laugh with you?"

Carl had no desire to talk about his mother. "But if your dad comes home and you're not there…"

"He's used to that! I'm often out. Dad never worries. You don't need to either." Since her mother had died, and they had lost one income, Schascha's father often worked long hours and overtime at the metalworking plant. The alternative was moving house—something he did not wish to put his daughter through. She couldn't lose her friends too. That was one thing he felt he could preserve.

"I'm going to go with you today. I've decided. I want to know what houses you visit. I only see you on Münsterplatz, then you disappear. I've often pictured where you go. Literally pictured. Proper drawings! And now I want to know. Because I'm curious. And one day I was so curious, I just decided to join you."

They were almost at Darcy's villa.

"Have you ever heard the saying 'Curiosity killed the cat'?"

Schascha stared at him, her eyebrows raised.

"In short, for you it means you're not coming with me. And that's my final word."

★ ★ ★

The following evening, she was back. Schascha had devised a cunning plan. Whatever ingenious arguments she presented for accompanying Carl, he always had a better counterargument. So she would say nothing, and simply tag along.

With every step, Carl waited for the words which never came. And as he had no idea what to say to her, he said nothing. They walked a while together, and Carl decided to allow her to accompany him because she was being so quiet, but only for today and even though he was convinced it was a mistake. He glanced at her.

"Not a single word. You stay completely silent!"

"Course."

"And don't do anything silly. Like children do."

"I never do."

"No annoying my customers."

"I never annoy anyone."

"I'm making an exception. Just for today! Do you know what an exception is?"

"Course. I'm not a kid anymore. I'm nearly ten!"

Schascha had to take two and a half steps for every one of Carl's, her stride uneven next to his, and the steady beat of his leather soles was replaced by an arrhythmic tempo as they walked together.

Mr. Darcy's villa appeared, and Carl stopped to take a deep breath.

"Mr. Darcy is a very good customer. He reads a book almost every day."

"A whole book?"

"Yes."

"Wow." Schascha gave a nod of respect. "I guess he doesn't do much else." She looked up at the villa. "The house must be full of books, right up to the roof!" A villa full of books sounded like paradise to her—or at least, the kind of paradise she was capable of imagining. It was not her classic paradise with candy floss trees and chocolate fountains, but Schascha was certain a nine-year-old should be allowed an entire collection of paradises.

"I don't think Mr. Darcy is very good with children," warned Carl as he rang the bell. At that precise moment, he felt a distinct affinity with the man.

The gentleman of the house opened the door, and immediately closed it again, having seen only Schascha and assuming she was collecting for charity. Darcy hated making personal donations. While he transferred a tenth of his annual income to the accounts of charitable organizations, placing money directly into a person's hand felt too much like almsgiving.

Carl rang the bell again. "It's me, Mr. von Hohenesch. Carl Kollhoff, from the City Gate bookshop."

Once more, the door opened. "What does the child want?"

"She's keeping me company. She's very well-behaved." It was more of a command toward her than a statement to him.

"How many books do you have?" Schascha piped up. "Altogether?"

Darcy shook his head as though he didn't quite understand the question.

"I'm good at counting," Schascha assured him, darting past him. "In fact, I'm very good at counting. Who says girls can't do math? So dumb! Like saying girls can't do sports. I can run and count at the same time! Shall I show you?" Schascha didn't wait for an answer. In her experience, the answer could sometimes be the wrong one. So she simply ran into the villa, which seemed to consist entirely of stairways and balustrades, doors and windows, and velvet-lined hallways hung with paintings. What it did not consist of was people—or books. Schascha had expected to see walls lined with book spines, but there was not a single one in evidence.

"Stop there, child!" a voice called behind her, but she pretended it was directed at some other person currently running through the villa.

She arrived at a vast empty room containing a fire in an old fireplace, a dark brown leather sofa, and a marble table, on which lay three books and a notebook.

"Three?" she exclaimed. "Only three? Where are all the others? In the cellar?" Schascha set off again, but her way was blocked by Darcy and Carl entering the room.

"I do apologize," said Carl. "I hadn't expected behavior like this." He truly was deeply ashamed. He handled his loyal customers—the few who were left—like delicate eggshells, and now he would be forced to watch as Schascha smashed one of them. And of all the people she could have chosen, she had picked Mr. Darcy, the most reserved of them, the man who guarded his privacy so meticulously. Why had Carl not remained firm; why had he let her come with him? He was such a stupid old man! He'd take this child straight home, wait there until her father came home from work, and tell him to make sure Schascha never bothered him again. Mr. Darcy took a step toward Schascha. What would his anger make him do?

"You won't find any other books," he said, his voice unexpectedly warm. "There are only these three in the house."

Schascha gazed at the fireplace in horror. "You burn them?"

Darcy sat down on the sofa. "Please, come over here."

Schascha complied without the slightest hesitation. She still inhabited a world where rich people must be good people; otherwise they would not be rich—a perspective that would undoubtedly alter with the years.

"You see, I love books, so I would never burn them. I do believe burning books should be permitted, although only in exceptional circumstances—to warm oneself in a bitterly cold winter, when faced with the threat of freezing to death. That could save lives. Books have many ways to do that: they can warm our hearts, and—in an emergency—our bodies too."

"But where are all your books then?" asked Schascha.

"Do you know, people are increasingly neglecting to read? And yet between those covers, you'll find people, their stories. Within each book lies a heart that begins to beat when someone reads it, because it makes a connection with the reader." Darcy's voice sounded sad. He didn't look at Schascha as he spoke, but stared into the fire. He didn't often speak much, and only succeeded in doing so now because it felt like speaking to himself. If he was speaking to anyone there, it was Carl, the man he had long wished to tell a great many things. "I am an anachronism, and content to be so. I am a slow-moving object in an ever-accelerating world. And I do so want people to read." Darcy picked one of the books from the modest pile. "Everything I read is taken directly to the old city library, for others to enjoy before the paper degrades."

"Degrades…" Schascha let the word slide over her lips. "Disgusting word. Sounds kind of sticky."

"Exactly! And infectious, like a disease you catch by touching the pages. No one wants to pick up a degraded book. It's like a person with leprosy. I have given the old city library money to fund an annex for degraded books, where they will be protected from further decay. A colony of outcasts, if you will. Sadly, there will never be healing for them."

Schascha pictured the old books huddling together in the dark library, but the sadness she felt was not only for them. The emptiness of this villa, with its bare, cold walls, saddened her too.

"But there must be some books you especially liked. They're

the ones you never want to give away—you want them with you always. I'd never give away *The Parent Trap!*"

"Those books which lie closest to our hearts are precisely the books we should give away, so that they may bring others happiness."

"You sound like a priest."

Darcy smiled. "Sometimes I feel like one." He turned to Carl. "Your companion is very astute."

"I'm as surprised as you."

"Do bring her again. But now I must attend a little more to my work; the stock exchanges in lands afar are about to close." Darcy preferred an antiquated turn of phrase; it lent his prosaic dealings with money a more charming air. "Next time, shall I show you my garden? You and Mr. Kollhoff. It's something I've wanted to show him for a long time."

Carl was not easily moved to tears. The last time he'd cried, he'd been fourteen years old, and his heart had just been broken by a girl to whom he'd written a love letter, scented with his mother's expensive perfume. She'd read it aloud to her friends before throwing it into the trash can. Carl couldn't recall her name now, but since that day, his tear ducts had lost the art of crying with sorrow. The sensation currently prickling the corners of his eyes must be dust irritation.

Mr. Darcy accompanied them to the door, where they made their farewells.

Carl stared hard at Schascha, while she concentrated on balancing on one leg. Time ticked by. Finally, she found her balance. "I know what you're going to say. I shouldn't have run in there. And you're right. I shouldn't."

Carl nodded.

"And you'll tell me you'd have liked to drag me out of there by the ear back to my dad." She raised a stern finger. "And I should never, ever, ever come back!"

Carl did not nod.

"But now the man was so nice, and invited us in, you can't say that anymore. Because that was a good thing I did—running in there—even if it was wrong. That's why you don't know what to say. Because you've got two voices in your head, and you've no idea which one is right. I'll make you a deal: I'm allowed to keep walking with you. And I'll behave. Because then I'll have learned from my mistake, and that's something that should be rewarded, right?"

"You seem to have thought it all through very thoroughly."

"It all popped into my head on the way down that long hallway."

"I have to get going," said Carl, setting off with a shake of his head. "The other books in my backpack need to go to their people."

"What about me?" asked Schascha. "I don't know how to get home from here!"

Carl stopped. "Did that come to you in the long hallway as well?"

Schascha nodded proudly. "Just in case the other reasons weren't enough."

Carl took a deep breath. "No more running into anyone's home? Not even if you're curious?"

"Nope, I won't."

"Honestly?"

Stepping forward, Schascha held out her hand, hooking her little finger around Carl's. Her smiling face was a picture of innocence.

"Pinkie promise." She shook their hands up and down to the beat, and the promise was sealed.

Their next point of call was to a nun who never set foot outside her convent. Five hundred and nineteen years after the foundation of her Benedictine order, the Vatican had decided it should be dissolved. One nun, however, had refused to leave. It was, after all, her home.

When Sister Maria Hildegard was born, no one could have guessed she would one day live in a convent. Her father was a molecular biologist, her mother an astrophysicist. Both had held a devout faith in science. Anything requiring words, not numbers, to explain, was of no value to them. God had never been invited into their lives.

Their daughter, on the other hand, began expressing her future career intentions by the time she was in kindergarten: not to be a princess or an astrobiologist (which was the unspoken dream of her parents), but to be a nun. Her parents had laughed, believing it a passing fad she would grow out of. Besides, they wanted grandchildren, as they often reminded her. But as their daughter grew, so did the desire. It was an unformed desire—much like a cloud, which cannot be grasped and has no fixed form, but is shaped by the wind. The cloud's appearance continually shifts, but it always remains the same cloud. After taking her Abitur exams, the daughter had traveled to Zimbabwe to work for six weeks with orphaned children. Coincidentally, the project was run by a Benedictine order. Working among the nuns brought peace into the life of the future Sister Maria Hildegard. She spent her evenings reading the New Testament—not as she had done in school, as homework to be completed before the next class, but of her own free will, and only as much as she could absorb in one sitting. She met a young man named Jesus, who showed her a way they could be together forever. The way led to a Benedictine convent. For the first time in her life, she felt as though she belonged. It was like coming home after believing herself homeless. Having found such a special place, Sister Maria Hildegard had no wish to ever leave; after all, life outside had never treated her so kindly.

The archdiocese had so far issued an eviction notice, cut off the electricity, water, and heating, and even threatened administrative fines. Unfortunately, under ancient ecclesiastical law, they were not permitted to remove her by force. If she left of her own volition, on the other hand, she could be prevented from reentering. Although Sister Maria Hildegard had no idea whether or not she was under constant surveillance, she did not wish to take any chances. Carl made regular deliveries of crime fiction. To each package, he would add a half kilo of flour and a pack of candles. They never spoke of it. Others in the neighborhood also made a habit of frequently dropping off a little something, in the hope that heaven might not look too unkindly on them for it.

Carl was not aware of the small kitchen garden in the convent courtyard, carefully tended by Sister Maria Hildegard. Nor was he aware of the well which supplied her with drinking water. He had no idea that the reason she spoke so knowledgeably about the weather was because of the great significance it had for her plants. He had given her the name of the pious monk from Hermann Hesse's *Narcissus and Goldmund*, although he had preferred to use the botanical umbrella term, calling her Sister Amaryllis.

Schascha was fascinated to meet a nun. She wanted to know whether nuns only ate wafers, whether they had hair under their veils (and what was the customary length for a nun), and whether there were special nun pajamas. She skipped the question of whether everything had to be washed in holy water in favor of another that was burning the tip of her tongue.

"Is it true nuns aren't allowed to marry?"

"Oh, but I am married."

"Oh? Does God know?"

Amaryllis laughed. "God is my bridegroom."

"Your bridegroom lives a long way away then."

"How so? Heaven is right above us."

"Maybe. But you can't fly." She scrutinized Amaryllis's habit closely. "Can you?"

"I've never tried."

"Try it sometime. If you're God's wife, he must want you with him."

"All nuns are married to God."

Schascha tilted her head. "I thought you were only allowed one wife." Then she nodded, as the answer dawned on her. "Of course, he's God, he doesn't have to keep to his own rules."

Sister Amaryllis was lost for words, and Carl swiftly said their goodbyes, as a way of pretending he hadn't noticed.

The next meticulously wrapped book was destined for Doctor Faustus: a man who claimed to be a professor emeritus, but who had in fact not had so much as a high school education. He had been intelligent enough, but his parents had had no money for his schooling, and so he had followed in his father's and grandfather's footsteps, becoming a railway conductor and subjecting himself each working day to unreasonable complaints from passengers over unpunctuality, incompetence, or surliness. An air of persecution hung perpetually over him. And he had an immense fear of dogs, particularly poodles. Yet he wished with all his heart for a loyal companion, a smart, faithful, distinguished dog, appropriate for an intellectual such as himself. It was a contradiction even he, with all his perspicacity, was unable to resolve.

Finding a name for him had been almost too easy. Doctor Faustus read historical treatises, with the sole purpose of refuting them on as many points as possible, in as many letters as possible to the authors or their universities. He would explain them all to Carl, although usually without context. His explanations also had a tendency to peter out, like rivers that divide too often and never return to their original course. At some point, the doctor would then close the door with a shake of his head.

Mrs. Longstocking had an unfortunate typing error for him ("writing in agony").

In between deliveries, Carl always felt particularly at one with himself and the world. Very little ran through his mind; even thinking about his route was a responsibility taken by his feet. Today was different. Although Schascha did not say much, she was there, and that changed everything.

Why was she there? Carl suddenly wondered, first in his head, then out loud.

"Why don't you play with other children? Don't they do that anymore?"

"Yeah, they do."

"But not you?"

"Yeah, I do."

"But not now?"

"Nope."

"Don't you have any friends?"

"Course."

Carl was accustomed to monosyllabic exchanges with work experience students. Not a single word too many. Perhaps they were saving energy for other activities.

"Who then?"

"Alex, Leila, Simone, Anna, Eva-Lina, Tim. No, not Eva-Lina, not anymore. She's a stupid, arrogant doofus. Can I hand over the next book?"

Carl loved the moment of handing over a book, wrapped like a gift. Though he would never have admitted it, it made him feel a little—a very little—like Father Christmas. "No, that's not possible."

"Please! Just once!"

"Sorry, no."

"Pleasepleasepleasepleaseplease!"

"Maybe another time, but not for Effi Briest." She was the last call on his round today.

"No, now! Then I won't bother you anymore. Promise."

"That's blackmail."

"I know. Is it working?"

Effi Briest's house appeared ahead of them. Carl shook his head. "No. But you can ring the bell."

"That's not the same thing at all!"

"Unlike handing over the book, it makes a pleasant sound." This was true; the bell played the Westminster chimes.

After a short pause, Effi opened the door, slightly out of breath. "Hello, Mr. Kollhoff." She caught sight of Schascha. "Have you brought your granddaughter today?" She held out her hand in greeting.

"No, I'm Schascha. I'm helping him. You should always help old people!"

Carl felt old every day, but never had he felt so old as at that moment. Schascha might as well have hung a sign around his neck that said "Can't Manage Alone."

"I love children," said Effi.

"Do you have any?" To Schascha, it was a simple question, requiring a one-word answer: yes or no. For Andrea Cremmen, the reply was not a word. It was not even a book. It was a whole library.

"Not yet," she summarized.

Carl unbuckled the backpack and untied the cord to pull out the final book of the day.

"Can I hand it over?" asked Schascha in a voice dripping with honey.

"Do let the child hand the book over. It seems to mean so much to her."

Carl hesitated. For the first time in decades, he would not complete a book delivery. Everything was changing, and it was changing much too quickly for Carl. The muscles in his hands protested, stopping midway to Schascha's small fingers.

Finally, she reached out and took the package, pressing it much too quickly and unceremoniously into Effi's hands.

"Unwrap it! I always tear my presents open super quickly, 'cause I want to see what's inside!" Schascha laughed. "Now I want to see what's in yours."

It was *Daughter of the Shadow Rose*, sequel to the bestselling novel. According to the back cover, it followed the continuing dramatic saga of a young girl who had grown up in a cruel orphanage and developed an extraordinary talent for gardening.

"It looks very sad," said Schascha, studying the cover illustration of a woman striding across a moor, her head bowed against a storm.

Effi leafed through the pages. "It is, but it's also very true to life. At any rate, I'm looking forward very much to reading it." She looked back at Schascha. "Will you bring me another book sometime?"

"Of course," replied Schascha, "if he lets me."

"You will let her, won't you?"

Carl smiled. "We'll see."

Effi glanced back at Schascha. "For Mr. Kollhoff, that means yes."

It meant no, and Effi suspected as much. But she didn't want it to mean no, and as long as a thing was not articulated clearly, there was room for interpretation, which it would be wrong not to exploit.

They said their goodbyes, and Carl was then obliged to accept the next alteration to his precise routine, since he would have to take Schascha back to Münsterplatz instead of heading directly home. As a result, he would have less time at home to read, would read fewer pages, would require a longer time to finish his book—all of which would mean a delay to beginning the next book. When every part of a life meshed together like the finest clockwork, even the tiniest dust particle could wreak havoc with the mechanism.

"She's a nice lady," said Schascha, who had decided to walk backward for a while. "But there's something not right about her."

"I know."

"It was funny, the way she flicked through the book. Did you notice?"

"What do you mean?"

"I don't know. I'll have to watch her more carefully next time. Something about the way she did it wasn't normal."

"Effi is a singular person."

Schascha switched to hopping. "Why do you call them Effi Briest and Mr. Darcy? They have completely different names on their doorbells."

"Those are my names for them—more appropriate names. People who love reading deserve to have a literary name."

"Do I deserve one?"

"Do you read a lot?"

"Enough to get a name!"

"What name would you give yourself?"

"I asked you first!"

Carl hesitated. "No, you didn't."

Schascha laughed. "Okay, you're right. But you can give me a name tomorrow, okay? Bye-bye, Book Walker!" With that, she was gone.

Carl decided to buy a bottle of wine: he suddenly felt the need to soothe his nerves. Just as vintage cars needed a little grease now and then, so Carl needed wine. It had to be a Franconian Silvaner, not just for the pear and quince notes, but also for the pleasure of running his fingers over the wonderfully rounded shape of the Bocksbeutel bottle—a distinctive shape almost unique to the wine region.

He bought two bottles. After all, Schascha was likely to turn up again tomorrow.

The following day, Carl went to visit Gustav Gruber, his former boss, at the Münsterblick care home. Although the name meant Minster View, the minster would only have been visible had the residents been capable of scaling the gabled roof and leaping three meters into the air. Carl always visited Gustav between breakfast and lunch. It was important not to disturb him at mealtimes. In a care home, time is measured in meals, not hours, with the day further punctuated by afternoon coffee and cake, supper, and finally a nightcap with something sweet.

In his younger years, Gustav had had wheaten-blond curls. They were still the same color now, albeit from a less natural source. Their intensity seemed to mock the last wisps of eyebrow and the ash-gray chin stubble. Gustav had the slight air of a clown who had long since removed his makeup. Humor still glowed from his laughter lines, and intelligence still nestled in the thoughtful furrows on his forehead. The roguish twinkle in his eye may have faded to a glimmer, but the old man still had a few last tricks up his sleeve.

Gustav lay in the bed, a book in his hand. He'd taken the paper cover off. Although he could barely hold the weight of a hardback book, he couldn't abide paperbacks. Only a hardcover felt protective enough for the valuable words inside, keeping them safe from harm. Now that he felt so unprotected himself, with Time and Death gnawing at his every extremity, he wanted security at least for the words that acted as his companions for this brief time.

As Carl entered, Gustav pushed the book under the covers.

"You're looking well," said Carl.

"Not your best lie ever. I don't ever look well these days! If I were a house, the demolition crew would have arrived long ago."

Carl pointed to the bed cover. "You do this every time, Gustav."

"What? Look unwell? I've been practicing that for years!"

"Hiding the book."

"There'll be a reason for that then, won't there?"

"Do you think I care whether you're reading porn, at your age?"

Gustav barked a laugh, which ended in a cough. Since that had begun to happen, he had tried to give up laughing, and had ceased to read, watch, or listen to anything humorous as a result. He would throw away the cartoon pages in the newspaper without reading them. This had succeeded in reducing his coughing fits, but his lungs missed laughter. It had always improved his circulation. His heart missed it all the more.

"I'm so old," said Gustav, when he could catch his breath again, "I wouldn't even understand the stuff they write in books like that. I'm so old, erotic novels are Ancient Greek to me. I might be able to read the letters, but the meaning is lost!"

"Then why do you always hide your book?" Carl sat on a chair next to Gustav's bed, and squeezed his hand.

"You really want to know what I'm reading?"

"Of course."

"You'll laugh!"

"I won't, I promise."

He drew the book out and held it out to Carl: *Treasure Island*. Carl stroked the cover, admiring the quality of the cloth binding.

"I'm reading the books from my youth. Adventure novels. Lots of Karl May. I've noticed much of the writing is not as great as I remembered it, but it still feels like coming home."

"And you're ashamed of that? You daft old fool!"

"The carers here call me the Professor, because I'm a bookseller. *Was* a bookseller..." He faltered. "They think I'm an intellectual. Me! Can you imagine?"

"But you are."

"Reading a lot doesn't make you an intellectual, any more than eating a lot makes you a gourmet. I'm an egotist, reading purely for my own pleasure, out of love for good stories, not to learn something about the world."

"There's no way to completely avoid learning. Something will lodge now and then, even in an old head like yours."

Gustav tapped *Treasure Island* with his finger. "My parents gave me these books back then. You know they were booksellers too."

"The Gruber dynasty."

"Exactly! Some families show their love with food—an extra thick layer of butter on your bread, or a second slice of wurst on top. Others hold each other close and often, sharing warmth to keep the cold of the outside world at bay. For generations, my family have shown their love through books. It doesn't even have to suit the recipient. When I started school, I struggled to decode even a single sentence. I would stumble over the pronunciation of each letter, then string them clumsily together." He laughed, setting off another cough. "Believe it or not, that was when my father gave me Thomas Mann's *Buddenbrooks*! Hundreds of pages full of long sentences! Wonderful sentences, words forged together like exquisite gold chains, but so long that their greatest impact was to frighten me. A year later, Tolstoy's *War and Peace* followed, and when I turned ten, and had yet to lose any time, my mother gave me Proust's *À la recherche du temps perdu*. To my parents, there were no books for children or adults, just good or bad books, and they gave me the best, like others give diamond jewelry that you keep for a lifetime." Gustav grinned. "Have I been lecturing you again?"

"I've known you my whole life, and I wouldn't have you any other way."

"Liar!" He punched Carl's arm. It had all the power of a gentle breeze. "But don't stop!"

"I've just finished reading a book that made me think of you."

"Was it about a notorious womanizer who, even at his advanced age, chases every skirt he sees?" His dull eyes took on a teasing sparkle.

"It was about an old bookseller who traveled to all the places he'd read about."

Gustav sat up a little straighter in the bed. It took a great deal of effort. Then he gestured to his gaunt body. "Do I look in a fit state for traveling to you? Just getting to the toilet feels like an expedition." He gave Carl a warm smile of understanding. "You're a bookseller to your bones, aren't you? Never ask me how I am, just recommend books to me."

"I learned that from you." He handed *Treasure Island* back. "Maybe Stevenson's novel would be the thing to persuade our new work experience lad to read."

"Sabine told me about him. Leon, isn't it?"

"You'd have found the perfect book for him long ago. It's times like this we miss you most."

Gustav brushed his words aside. "One day, Sabine will be able to do that much better than I ever could."

Carl's chair was suddenly uncomfortable, and he wriggled to find a better position. There was none.

"Touchy subject for you? Now you're the old fool!" Gustav gave a wry smile. "I know you won't believe me, but Sabine is very fond of you, even if she's not good at showing it."

"I'm fond of her too. She's your daughter, after all."

"And your boss!"

"Exactly. I'm contractually obliged to be fond of her."

"You just need to understand, she wants to do everything differently—better. That's the prerogative of youth." He smoothed the bed cover. "And she needs to assert herself in front of the others. A boss can't show weakness." He leaned forward, and lowered his voice to a whisper. "She's promised me you can continue delivering books as long as you want."

"Thank you." Carl didn't look him in the eye. He didn't want to show Gustav how much delivering books meant to him, even though the old man had long been well aware.

"She's always been a little envious of you," Gustav continued, "because you're the natural-born bookseller, and she isn't."

He was wrong. His daughter had always believed her modern methods to be superior. She had also always sensed that Carl occupied a special place in her father's heart. She may have envied Carl's skill, but she envied the love all the more.

"People trust you," Gustav was saying. "That's the most important thing for a bookseller. When you recommend a book, the customer doesn't just hope they'll enjoy it—they're certain of it. And if they don't enjoy it, it must be their own fault, not yours." He winked.

"I'm supposed to be cheering you up, not the other way around," said Carl.

"Well, I'm better at it, so I'm taking over the task!"

Carl decided it was time for their little quiz. They played it on every visit, with a new subject each time. "Name the five best books...for cheering someone up."

Gustav nominated five, then Carl listed his candidates. They discussed the strengths and weaknesses of each book, and the authors. Then they moved on to the best books in which a character lived in a care home. That was a trickier task, but they cracked it in the end. Carl said Gustav should come back to the bookshop, if only for a few hours a week. Gustav laughed far too much. Eventually, he ran out of breath.

"I won't ever come back, you know that," said Gustav.

"Don't say that."

"We're old valve radios, you and I. Our time is past. We don't notice it while we're still functional, but we can't get the replacement parts."

"You sound like one of those greeting cards with their inspirational quotes."

"That's not so bad; they sell well!" Gustav wheezed. "I need a nap. It's good for my youthful complexion!" He hesitated. A lurid splash of pain came over his face. This was the point in the conversation where he always asked the same question. This time, he needed to take a deep breath, and his voice trembled as the words came out. "Will you come again next week?"

"Of course."

"It's good to hear that."

"I'll keep on visiting you for years yet, you know that."

Gustav nodded and turned his head away.

"Take care, boss," said Carl, stroking Gustav's bony arm in farewell.

"Take care, young'un."

chapter 3

The Red and the Black

THE FRAMED NEWSPAPER ARTICLE about Carl had disappeared from the wall of the City Gate bookshop, the only evidence of its loss a pale rectangle on the textured wallpaper. In place of a greeting, Sabine Gruber met him with the words, "Carl, we're getting fewer and fewer orders for your round." Then she let out a sigh.

"I don't take much for the delivery service."

"But the logistical effort, Mr. Kollhoff!" She raised her eyebrows until they were almost touching her hairline. "It takes so much time, for so few books. We use a completely different system now."

"It makes them so happy." As he said it, Carl pictured in his mind's eye the grateful, smiling faces of his customers.

"It would make them even happier to walk the few steps into the shop. Exercise is good for people; so is fresh air! Don't you agree? So we no longer want to advertise this particular service. We won't tell our customers about it. I'm sure we agree on that, don't we, Mr. Kollhoff?"

He'd known Sabine since the day she was born. She'd sat on his knee while he read her book after book, or chanted "horsey, horsey" until she laughed. She'd called him Uncle Carl. Sabine had been one of the few children Carl had liked. When she took over the business, she'd called him into her office and told him that from now on, they would use a more formal mode of address when talking to one another; it was more appropriate, she insisted.

Carl didn't find it at all appropriate.

"You're the boss," he said. Looks of sympathy and encouragement from the bookshop's other employees followed him as he walked into the back office to wrap his books. Carl had taught the ropes to every single person working there. No one spoke; they were all lost for words.

Nick Hornby's *Fever Pitch* still lay unread on the desk; Leon still squatted unreading on the floor.

Silently, Carl wrapped his books. There was one for Hercules; it would be a longer walk today.

As he approached Münsterplatz, Carl slowed, glancing from side to side in search of a bouncing mop of dark hair to avoid. Today, he could do without a companion asking all the wrong questions—or even worse: all the right ones.

He was reluctant to take a different route across Münsterplatz, under the shade of the awnings, close to the shops, past the tables and chairs where people sat eating and drinking, but that was where Schascha was least likely to spot him. Carl even considered taking his hat off, but instantly dismissed the idea as absurd.

Just a few more steps, and he'd turn safely into Beethovenstrasse.

"You don't usually walk along here," a cheerful voice piped up beside him. "I almost didn't see you."

Carl looked at Schascha—and stopped in his tracks.

"Looks good, don't you think?" She twirled on the spot. "No yellow today, even though it's my favorite color!"

She was wearing olive green jeans, a T-shirt the color of a frog, and a pale green raincoat, accessorized with a backpack. The overall effect was of Carl in miniature, and Schascha had borrowed clothes especially from two friends to achieve it. Carl had been determined to tell her she couldn't come with him today, but at the sight of her clothing, he didn't have the heart.

"Don't girls of your age prefer wearing pink?" he asked.

"I'm almost ten!"

"Pardon me."

"I like spots, but I don't like checks, or squares, or anything with corners."

"You're not wearing any spots."

Schascha drew her trouser legs up a little, revealing spotted socks. "They're my trademark. What socks are you wearing? Show me."

"They don't have any spots." Carl didn't want to show his socks.

"I thought so. You don't look like a spots person."

"What does a spots person look like?"

"Not like you. Trust me, I know a lot about spots. Can we go? I've got plans!"

Carl stayed where he was. "What plans? I need to know. Are you going to run into someone's house again?"

"No, nothing bad, I promise! Cross my heart! But I won't tell you till I'm done."

"But—"

"I'm only doing it for you! Okay, not just for you—but

mostly." She looked up at him. "Actually, I have two great things planned, and I can tell you the second one. In fact, I need to tell you the second one!"

"I'm all ears." *All fears* would have been closer to the mark, but even in his current state of mild anxiety, Carl liked to remain polite.

"Last night, when I was in bed, I was thinking. I always think a lot before I fall asleep, when everything is dark—apart from the glow-in-the-dark stars on my ceiling, of course." She raised her index finger. "So, you can't think of a good bookcharacter name to give me, because you don't know me well enough. That's why today, I'm going to tell you lots and lots about myself. Everything, with any luck."

As they walked, Schascha proceeded to do exactly that. From her birth (just a two-hour labor; she had hair right from the start) to kindergarten (seals group; airplane picture on her coat hook) to school (Class A, the best; unfortunately, Ms. Schild wasn't the best teacher). She was not the most popular girl in Class A; quite the opposite. Not only was she the last one to be picked for team sports, and the one with whom nobody wanted to work in a group, but she was also the one who always spent break times sitting on the ground alone outside the caretaker's office window, while the others in her class played catch, or climbed on the equipment. Schascha emphasized at every opportunity how much she loved books, and that the other children teased her, calling her a bookworm. They had also drawn an actual worm on her chair using a felt-tip pen—and not just any worm, but a worm going to the toilet. Even Simon laughed at her, and he looked like Ron Weasley, took no interest in anything that wasn't a computer game, and thought all girls were losers. Schascha didn't think he was a loser, not at all, though she couldn't explain why.

And she certainly didn't know what to do with the strange feeling *that* gave her.

The first stop on their round today was at a fashionable apartment building that was home to Hercules.

"Just a second," said Schascha, before Carl could press the bell next to the name Mike Tröffer. She began awkwardly pulling an enormous friendship album from her backpack. It was covered in unicorns and rainbows, and secured on one side with a combination lock. While Carl knew that books could save the world, he was one of the very few who knew this was just as true of friendship albums. The world they could save might be small, but to whoever lived in that world, it was the only one that mattered.

"You mustn't run in," warned Carl. "He'll invite us into the kitchen for a cup of tea, in any case."

"I've already promised I won't run into anyone's house. Only Mr. Darcy's. And that was a good thing!"

"Must you always have the last word?"

"Am I right or not?"

At that moment, the outer door opened. They climbed to the second floor to find a muscular man waiting at his apartment door, immense muscles bulging from his black T-shirt.

"Mr. Kollhoff, come in! I'll just put the Earl Grey tea on for you."

"Do you really like that weird tea?" whispered Schascha, looking up at Carl.

"No, but it would be impolite to tell him."

"But then you always have to drink tea you don't like."

"His hospitality is compensation for it."

Hercules shook Carl's hand, then Schascha's. She felt a moment of fear as his huge paw closed over her tiny hand, but Hercules gave it the gentlest squeeze. "I'm Mike, and you are...?"

"Schascha."

"Do you like Earl Grey tea too?"

"No, I don't."

Hercules led them into the kitchen. "Water? Milk?"

"I don't mind." Schascha gazed around, open-mouthed. She had never seen an apartment like this. The white plastered walls were hung with silver-framed pictures of word art: block letters hung next to calligraphy so ornamented, it was barely decipherable; there were quotes written into the shape of a heart, and others shaped to look like a church.

The white-and-silver theme continued into the kitchen, which was so clean and tidy, you might have thought it was newly installed that day. Schascha asked if she might use the bathroom, and Hercules showed her the way.

When she returned, a glass of chilled water stood ready on the table for her, and Carl was accepting his steaming tea. Hercules drank nothing.

"Before I take a sip, I must deliver your book," said Carl, drawing it from the Bundeswehr backpack.

Hercules unwrapped it with a care Schascha had not observed in any of Carl's other customers. He stroked it with a reverence verging on religious devotion. She scribbled a rapid note in her album.

"It's exactly the rare edition you wanted," said Carl. He had succeeded in purchasing it from an antiquarian bookseller, but still could not fathom why Hercules had ordered such a valuable copy.

Schascha craned her neck to read the title.

"*The Sorrows of Young Werther?* Is that like—"

"No," interrupted Carl.

"But you don't know what I was going to say!"

"Yes, I do. Trust me. It's a question I've heard too many times for my taste."

"Too many times for it to be original?" She grinned.

"I think we understand one another."

Hercules handed the novel back to Carl. "Tell me about the book, Mr. Kollhoff!"

"I don't want to give too much away."

"No, you must, right to the end. Give me the whole nine yards."

Their conversation always followed the same path, like a small rhetorical dance, so different from those routines that Carl habitually stepped into. As usual, Carl demurred a little, in the hope that Hercules would change his mind. But his customer remained adamant each time, so Carl gave in.

"It's an epistolary novel, in which the young Werther, a law student, is hopelessly in love with Lotte, who is engaged to another man."

"How does Werther fall in love with her?" asked Hercules, his brow creasing.

"Right from the first moment he sees her cutting bread for her younger siblings. He's moved by her motherliness. She's also very beautiful."

"Motherliness," repeated Hercules. "And Werther? What kind of man is he?"

"A tempestuous fellow. The novel is also regarded as belonging to the Sturm und Drang literary movement."

"And Lotte's fiancé?"

"Albert is conservative and traditional."

"A stuffed shirt." Hercules nodded. "And how does it all turn out in the end? Does Werther get his Lotte?"

Carl shook his head, recalling how affected he'd been the first time he'd read the novel. It was a pain that remained with him. "Sadly, no. When he kisses her, Lotte flees to an adjoining room. Werther decides to kill himself to avoid besmirching Lotte's honor. At midnight the night before Christmas

Eve, he shoots himself in the head, and dies of his injuries the following day."

Hercules clapped his hands together. "Wow! Blockbuster ending! What sort of weapon was it?"

"That he used to...?"

"Exactly."

"Oh, I'll have to pass on that. I only know it was a pistol that he borrowed from Albert."

"Harsh."

"It gets harsher: because Werther commits suicide, he cannot have a Christian burial. It's the worst punishment, so to speak."

"Brutal!"

"I'm certain you'll enjoy it."

Hercules stretched his neck until it cracked. "Yeah, I'm a big reading fan! And this book is real important, everyone should read it, you said so yourself. Next time, what about something by a Nobel Prize winner, Mr. Kollhoff?"

Carl checked his watch. It had stopped working over twenty years ago, but he loved the way it sat so comfortably on his wrist. "I'm afraid it's time I was going. I have other people eagerly awaiting their books." He passed the *Werther* over.

"Yeah, of course. Thanks for always taking the time here with me."

"It's my pleasure, and I mean that with all my heart. It's a great joy to see someone so enthusiastic about the classics of literature."

Hercules's smile had a touch of embarrassment, Schascha thought. On the other hand, she had little exposure to smiles on a face as muscular as this one; perhaps they always looked like that.

Outside the door, she made a few more notes in her friendship album, then opened her mouth to say something to Carl. For the first time ever, Carl was faster. "You don't need to tell me there's something peculiar here." He looked around for Dog, who often joined him here, but the animal was nowhere to be seen. "I know already. I just can't put my finger on what."

"All his books are red," replied Schascha.

"What do you mean?" Carl set off again at his usual pace.

"I sneaked into his living room when I said I needed to go to the bathroom. I didn't need to at all!" Her little chin stuck out proudly.

"Aren't you a slyboots?"

"I saw his bookcase in there. All his books have red... What's that thing called at the side? Not the side that opens, the other side."

"Spine."

"They were all red!"

"Unusual. Although I do have a customer with a marked dislike of one particular color."

"There were only three colors in the whole living room: black, white, and red! Except the films, well, the film spines on the cases, they were different colors, and the CDs. I'll have to look more closely next time."

"Are you going to explain to me now what all this has to do with your friendship album?"

"I'm putting all your customers in it." She opened it awkwardly. "I got it in second grade, but there are still lots of blank pages." Many of her classmates had given the book back without writing anything in it, or worse still, with messages she had promptly torn out. "You're supposed to stick photos at the top," she explained, "but I can't ask your customers to do that. That's why I've brought some colored pencils, so I can draw them, though I'm not very good at it."

Carl glanced through the album, reading the sections aloud. "Favorite color? Favorite band? Favorite teacher?"

"I'm doing it differently," declared Schascha. "I'm writing

down the titles of important books, and what it looks like in the places where people live, and what it smells like. Things like that."

"How will you find all that out? Are you planning a series of interrogations?"

"What are interrogations?"

Carl pondered. "When you fire a lot of questions at someone."

"But when someone asks questions, it means they're interested in you. It's nice. If I ask questions, I mean it nicely." She tucked the album back into her little backpack.

"You have to permit the other person to ask questions as well. Otherwise it's not a conversation."

Schascha didn't understand what Carl meant. If someone asked questions, they got answers—that was then a conversation.

Suddenly, Dog was there, its tail erect, winding around, past, between their legs. It looked like the kind of dance that was once performed long ago in large, magnificent ballrooms.

For the first time, Schascha noticed that Carl gave the cat something to eat: a slice of peeled Fleischwurst, which he unwrapped from a piece of sandwich paper.

"You're really clever, but giving it bologna is dumb."

Carl looked at her in astonishment. "Why? You can see how much Dog enjoys it."

"If you give it bologna, you won't know whether it comes for the bologna or for you."

"Perhaps it's a bit of both."

"But you don't know that. That would bother me. I wouldn't want a pet to come to me just because it wants something to eat."

"Dog isn't a pet. If anything, it's a street animal, a free spirit.

It comes because it wants to. I'm not interested in the reason. Some things are best left a mystery."

Schascha shook her head. "I'd want to know!"

"But Dog prefers it this way. Let it keep its little secret."

Schascha bent to stroke Dog. The cat stretched its head toward her, and Schascha was pleased that this token of affection at least was wholly on account of her stroking skills, and entirely non-bologna-related.

Mrs. Longstocking greeted them in high spirits with a cry of "Three shit in street gang frenzy!" then pressed a hand to her mouth to prevent a laugh escaping. "I bet you can't think of anything for that, Mr. Kollhoff, apart from the obvious!" Today, she was wearing matching shoes, with odd socks.

Carl scratched his temple. He could feel the expectant gazes of Mrs. Longstocking, Schascha, and even Dog, all directed at him. In his youth, he had battled his way through *Meyers Encyclopedia*, from *A* for *Aachen* to *Z* for *Zygospore*. It had configured his neural pathways during his developmental years to such an extent, he could now function as a living lexicon.

"This denotes a particularly dramatic form of criminality exclusively found in Mexico. The spiciness of the food typically found in this country has been increasingly shown to cause digestive problems. If bowel evacuation cannot be induced, there is a corresponding rise in rage. In Mexico, those afflicted traditionally run into the street, together with other sufferers, to vent their anger on greengrocers, particularly those selling beans. This collective physical activity can often have the desired effect on the digestive tract, for which reason street gang frenzies are an integral part of Mexican culture. They are considered a folk tradition, featuring in many songs and vividly described in numerous books."

Mrs. Longstocking gave a flamboyant bow. "You've given the obvious quite a lively twist."

"Mrs. Long—" Schascha closed her mouth abruptly, just in time.

"My name is Dorothea Hillesheim, but please, call me Thea—everyone does."

Schascha opened up her friendship album, holding an HB pencil (with eraser tip) at the ready.

"Why do you and Carl play this game creating new definitions for funny typos?"

"What do you mean?"

"Most people don't even notice them. I don't, anyway. Why do you?"

"You're very clever, do you know that?"

A proud smile stole across Schascha's face. "Course I know. But sometimes it's a dumb way to be."

"When other people notice?"

"You're trying to distract me, aren't you?"

"You're even cleverer than I thought." Mrs. Longstocking leaned forward to whisper in Schascha's ear, then spoke in a stage whisper so loud, even Carl could hear. "I've been an elementary schoolteacher my whole life. Now, even though I no longer work in a school, I'm still that same teacher. It's not something you can just shrug off." She straightened up.

"You mean the job grows roots inside you?"

"That sounds slightly uncomfortable," said Mrs. Longstocking, pulling a face. "It's more like a precious ring that I can't get over my knuckle anymore. Sometimes I can feel it's there, but usually I don't even notice it. It's only other people who point it out now."

Schascha's gaze dropped involuntarily to Mrs. Longstocking's hands. Judging by the old woman's wrinkled, ring-bedecked fingers, she must have taught a vast number of subjects during her career.

While Carl delivered his customer's order, Schascha made notes. She said nothing until they began walking away. Even then, she spoke quietly, as though Mrs. Longstocking could hear them through the closed door.

"I told a lie. I'm not clever at all."

"Oh, you are. Everyone makes mistakes, but that doesn't make you any less clever. In fact, it's the only way to really become clever at all."

"But I make a lot of mistakes. I might even have to repeat a school year."

"You'll have to study hard then."

"I know. But I feel like there are so many things that just won't fit into my brain." She banged her fist against her forehead until Carl gently grasped hold of her hand.

"There's a very simple trick for that."

"What's that?"

"You need to read more. It makes the brain flexible, so that anything can fit into it."

Schascha pondered Carl's words, but whichever way she looked at them, they made no sense. There was much about Carl and his customers that made no sense; that was what Schascha loved about them. All the TV programs for her age group made perfect sense, and she found them terribly dull. They gave the impression that the world held no more mysteries worth growing up for.

As they rounded a corner, the minster came into view, presenting the particularly splendid sight of its large round, multicolored rose window depicting the twelve apostles, and its one and a half towers stretching heavenward.

Turning a little away from Schascha so that she wouldn't see, Carl crossed himself.

"Why did you do that?" she piped up.

Carl sighed. "I cross myself whenever I see the main door of the minster."

"Because of God?"

"No, not because I'm a believer. I leave faith to those who are more expert in it than I. It's a mark of respect for the most powerful book in the world. A book that has sparked wars and forgiveness, great injustice and profound love. If you believe in the power of the written word—and I do—you can do nothing but take your hat off to this work, and take a deep bow. Metaphorically speaking." He tapped his hat. "This one, on the other hand, remains firmly on my head. For reasons of safety."

"You're funny."

"Who's funnier? The funny old man, or the girl keeping the funny old man company?"

"The funny old man, of course!"

Carl smiled. He knew he was funny, but it didn't feel like that to him. If a person is funny for long enough, it finally becomes normal, if only to himself.

It suddenly came to Carl's attention that his stride was changing. As he walked through the old city, his paces, ingrained in his muscle memory by decades of habit, were shortening to accommodate Schascha's shorter legs.

"Who are we going to now?" asked Schascha, tugging her backpack straps tight.

"To Effi. Mrs. Cremmen."

Schascha pointed down a dark alleyway, virtually devoid of daylight. A relic from medieval times, it had never been paved—with the exception of a few scattered areas of cobblestones—but remained clay soil, compacted by centuries of feet. "This is a great shortcut!"

"Sometimes the long path is better than the short one."

"Why?"

"You'll find out," said Carl. It was the standard adult response to a child when a better answer failed to spring to mind, but it made Carl uneasy, so he opted for the truth: "I'm a stupid old fool, and that alleyway frightens me. I don't know why, but I always shy away from it, like a horse shies away from a gravestone."

Schascha stopped, and wriggled her enormous friendship album out of her bag. Next, she produced a glitter-encrusted pen hung with brightly colored plastic tassels. It was her special pen for Carl. She began to scribble.

"Are you writing that I'm a horse?"

"No."

"Good."

"Just that you're a scaredy-cat."

Carl smirked. He hadn't been called that since his school days. With a rush of memory, he stood once again in front of the high bar in the gym, not daring to climb up. He had always believed children made it painfully clear how old you had become—now he realized that perhaps they also made it clear how young you have remained.

Schascha danced around Carl and Dog, who growled in irritation. "By the way, I know who Effi Briest was."

"Is," replied Carl.

"No, was. She lived a long time ago. And she died in the book."

"If you're a character in a book, you live forever. For as long as someone reads you, you're alive."

"In that case, I want to be in a book too!"

"You'll have to write your own then."

"Okay." Schascha ran ahead. "Yippee! I'm going to be a book writer!"

Carl didn't see her again until he reached Effi's house, where he found her sitting on the doorstep, slightly out of breath. "You took your time."

"But I enjoyed the journey. Have you rung the bell yet?"

"Nope, I've been waiting for you all this time." Schascha stood up and pressed the doorbell. "I've got a surprise planned," she whispered. Suddenly it struck Carl that Schascha's running and jumping could be ascribed to her anticipation of the surprise. He found the thought deeply unsettling.

Before he could inquire any further, Effi opened the door. "Hello, Mr. Kollhoff. Hello, Schascha. I was just hanging up laundry in the basement; it's lucky I heard the doorbell at all."

"Your book is by far the most substantial of the day," said Carl; it was not a complaint, but a means of igniting Effi's anticipation. Schascha made no move to hand over the book, so Carl did it himself, with a shrug. Schascha was already concentrating on what was to come next. She had imagined this moment in her mind's eye, painted in the same luminous colors she had used when creating the surprise for Effi. She bobbed up and down on her toes: jumping seemed inappropriate to the occasion.

"It's such a doorstop!" said Effi, puffing her cheeks out as she accepted the packet.

Carl smiled. "Every new book order ought to be delivered with the time necessary to read it."

"If you could include a small packet of that next time you come, I'd be very grateful!"

Effi unwrapped the book immediately. It was *The Shadow Rose Abroad*. To Schascha, it looked even sadder than the previous book in the series. It gave the impression that the publisher had attempted to squeeze as much condensed misery as possible between the covers, on paper manufactured with concentrated tears.

Schascha stepped forward, her heart pounding. "I've not

brought you a packet of time, but I have got this for you." She set her backpack down laboriously, and took out a sheet of paper, rolled up and tied with a red-and-gold gift ribbon. "For you, Mrs. Cremmen."

"What's this?"

"I'm not telling. Open it!"

Carl took a deep breath. This girl was such an unpredictable child! She looked so innocuous, yet the potpourri of things going on in her little head was anything but.

"It's a picture," said Effi, unrolling it. "A shadow rose…" she said, her voice trembling.

"It's growing in your house, Mrs. Cremmen. I don't know if you can see that very well. I get very low marks in art, which is totally unfair, but Mrs. Damian is super strict!"

Effi turned away to hide her tears. She had become so used to concealing her true feelings in recent years that it had become second nature. She hurriedly wiped the tears from her face. "Come in, let's find a good place to hang your picture."

It was the cheeriest house you could hope to imagine. Planters burgeoning with flowers stood everywhere, and pictures of blossoms covered the walls. The whole house appeared to be in bloom. It had clearly been built with two people in mind, yet it was equally clear that only one had left any trace of themselves. The living room table was occupied by a single book, the sink contained a single coffee cup, and the coat hook held a single jacket. And although there were numerous perfect places in the house for Schascha's picture, Effi hung it on the inside of the kitchen door, where it would only be seen when the door was closed.

Effi thanked Schascha effusively and gave her a bar of white chocolate. Carl was given one too, even though that kind of thing was not to his taste.

Once they stood outside again, Schascha began scribbling furiously in her friendship album.

Carl leaned closer. "Are you planning to get into all my customers' houses?"

"I have to, for my project!" she insisted.

And over the course of the following days, that was precisely what she did. She asked Mrs. Longstocking ("high stool studies") to correct her story-writing task (into which she had deliberately inserted a generous number of mistakes), she told the Reader her glasses were broken and she urgently needed him to read the final chapter of *Jim Button and Luke the Engine Driver* aloud to her (Schascha had picked the book because of its references to smoke; after all, he read aloud to women who rolled cigars). She begged Sister Amaryllis to hear her confession (and proceeded to tell her a hair-raising story of the theft of some Werther's Originals, while struggling to not laugh out loud). It took her three attempts to get into Doctor Faustus's home: he dismissed every historical artifact she brought as uninteresting, newfangled trash, even though her father's broken wristwatch was definitely very old, as was Grandma Ingrid's casserole dish with the floral pattern, and the packet of crispbreads that had been exposed to the sun for so long it had lost all its orange color, which was positively ancient. The day she presented the latter to him, he did, however, relent and invite her inside to show her something genuinely old: a couple of boring Roman coins.

And with that, the first part of Schascha's grand plan was complete.

The old cast-iron bench with its wooden slats looked built to host important conversations. In fact, many people had indeed talked together here: genuinely talked; listened to one another; tried to put themselves in the other's shoes. The bench stood in the city cemetery—the old part, with its huge, magnificent tombs from a bygone era, some resembling small chapels or Greek temples, others barred as if to hold utter darkness captive. Those who lay here had died long ago. The great oaks, the rampant brambles, and even the wildflowers planted here by the wind all suggested a soft resting place.

It was precisely this bench that Schascha had picked out for their conversation, and she now guided Carl toward it.

"We need to talk," she said in a serious tone as she sat down. She opened her friendship album as though the pages were made of thick card stock. "It's all in here!"

Carl laid one hand on top of the other on the wooden handle of his umbrella. "The things you wrote about my customers?"

Schascha gave a slow, earnest nod. "I've been thinking clever thoughts."

"That's the best type of thought."

Schascha took a deep breath, because what she was about to say needed to be announced in a full voice. "You need to take different books to your customers!"

Carl frowned—a facial expression he could make to great effect, since he had acquired a great deal of forehead over the years. "But I take them the books they order."

"They're all ordering the wrong ones."

"Aren't they the best people to know what they want?"

"Hah!" Schascha barked out a laugh. "Hah! I want to eat ice cream all day, but is that good for me? No!"

"But books aren't ice cream. They don't hurt your stomach."

"You don't understand!" Schascha would have stamped her feet, if only her legs could reach the ground.

"So you're saying I deliver the book equivalent of a stomachache?"

"Books are much, much more dangerous than ice cream! They hurt your head. Or worse, your heart." Schascha didn't know how she could make it any plainer to Carl. He was actually pretty smart, for an old man. How could he possibly not see it? Schascha tapped her finger firmly on her friendship album. "It's all in here! Your customers might order books, but it's not about the books at all!"

"No?"

"You need to look closer, Book Walker! The people smile when you arrive, but not when they're unpacking the books. You're much more important to them than the books. Maybe they know, deep down, that they're ordering the wrong books. Or do you think Effi needs sad books? She's got a sad enough life already!"

"It's her life. They're her books."

"Then isn't there a book that makes everyone happy? Like the Bible, but exciting?"

Carl twisted his umbrella as if he was chalking a snooker cue. "The Bible is exciting. Very exciting, in fact."

"Aaargh, you know what I mean! A book everyone will love."

Carl pushed his hat a little higher; his head seemed to be getting rather warm. "There's no such book. Years ago, I thought otherwise, and I gave everyone who was important to me the most wonderful book for Christmas. It had made me happy with every line, and I so wanted to share that happiness. But many didn't read it at all, or not to the end, or didn't enjoy it." Carl looked sadly at Schascha. It pained him to take her beautiful dream and destroy it. It was like bursting a beautiful, brightly colored bubble. "You see, there is no book that can please everyone. And if there were, it would be a bad book.

You can't be everyone's friend, because everyone is different. You'd have to be completely lacking in personality, no rough edges or sharp corners. But even then, many people wouldn't like you, because they need rough edges and sharp corners. Do you understand? Every person needs different books. Because what one person loves with all their heart, might leave another completely cold."

Schascha grinned with satisfaction. "Then we're agreed! We'll take everyone the book they need." She pointed to a page in her friendship album containing a painting of a weeping woman in the space for the photo. It was meant to represent Effi. "For example, she should get cheerful books. She'd at least read those to the end."

"How do you know she doesn't do that with the sad books?"

"She flips through the books when she unwraps them, but never to the end, like you would normally. I watched her very carefully! Then I went to her bookshelf and opened her books. You might not know this, but they automatically open up at the last place you've read to. It's really practical."

"I see. Good to know."

"They all fell open way before the end, fifty pages or more before. Some of the pages were still properly stuck together—they even creaked a bit when I opened them up." She turned the page and pointed to the next side. "Mrs. Longstocking is really anxious, she should get courageous books. And—"

"No," said Carl.

"No?"

"Yes. As in, no." Carl stood up.

"But why?"

"I refuse to patronize anyone. Everyone is free in their choice of books. That's the most marvelous thing about it. So much is dictated to us in life; at least we can still choose what we read."

Schascha stood, a tiny fizzing ball of rage. "But I've thought it all through: from now on, you have to take them the right books!"

"No." Carl shook his head. "Absolutely not."

chapter 4

Great Expectations

IN MUCH THE SAME way that a storm which begins brewing over a far distant ocean is inevitably destined to hit you in a few days' time, Carl had no idea what lay ahead. This was entirely due to the fact that, while his knowledge of foreign languages included English, French, Latin, and even a little Ancient Greek, it did not extend to the distinctly more complex language of Youth. Carl was unaware of the multiplicity of meanings the word *okay* could encompass. When Schascha said the word, Carl took it to mean, *Understood, they won't each be given a book they should read*. In fact, it had meant, *You can think that as much as you like, but I see it totally differently, and I'll do what I please, whatever you think*. The word *okay* was much bigger on the inside.

What didn't pass unnoticed was that the following day, Schascha's backpack had increased considerably in volume. The straps dug deep into her yellow winter jacket, and the weight was making her stand more upright than usual.

"Don't you want to drop off your school things at home first? I'll wait for you," said Carl.

"Nope, I'm fine."

"Should I carry something for you?"

"Absolutely not!" Schascha hunted for a good argument to stop Carl asking further questions. "You're old. I should be carrying something for you!"

Then Schascha asked who was getting a book today, and in what order. She'd never asked this before, but the question didn't strike Carl as strange in any way.

Their first customer was Mr. Darcy, who led them into the garden. It had rained, and Darcy, who was allergic to numerous types of pollen, felt able to step outdoors for a few hours. There was not another person in the city who longed so earnestly for a shower of rain: to him, each raindrop was a bead of pure, liquid freedom.

Inhaling a deep lungful of the purified air, he showed them his Linnaean floral clock, a flower bed from which they could interpret the time of day by its open blossoms. The noon flower bloomed from midday to 5:00 p.m., the night-flowering catchfly from 7:00 to 8:00 p.m., while the meadow goat's beard was the early riser, flowering from 3:00 a.m. to noon. Some plants were extremely precise: the gentian opened its buds at 9:00 a.m., the St. Bernard's lily at 6:00. As the year progressed, Darcy had a succession of new plants installed in the bed, as some only bloomed for a brief few weeks.

Next to the floral clock stood a magnificent basket chair. It looked as though it couldn't possibly have been woven by human hands, but had simply sprung from the garden's fertile soil, growing into a shape that promised the deepest comfort.

"You've got a beautiful reading seat there."

"It's not mine; no one has ever yet sat in that chair."

Carl stepped closer to the seat, and stroked his fingertips over its smooth, glossy material. "Is it an artwork?"

"No, it symbolizes a desire—or perhaps a dream. There is nothing I find more beautiful—please don't laugh at me—there is nothing I find more beautiful than a woman reading: when she sinks deep into a book and forgets everything around her, because she is actually somewhere else entirely. The movement of her pupils, the deep breathing at a particularly dramatic scene, or her smile at a humorous passage. I would so love to have a woman living here, whom I could watch as she reads all day." He smiled at himself. "It would be like reading a book in a language I don't understand. At university, there was a fellow student who often sat near me to read. Sadly, she had not the slightest interest in me."

Carl would have loved to hear more about this special fellow student, and about the floral clock, but there were books waiting to be delivered. Schascha was silent, repeatedly bouncing up and down on tiptoe. She was eager to move on, and had been right from the moment they had rung the doorbell.

Mildly aggrieved at Schascha's disinterest, Darcy escorted them back to the entrance, instead of watching the next flower open, as had been his plan.

For a few paces, Schascha said nothing, although she had the words assembled ready on her tongue. She was waiting until they were far enough from the villa before voicing them.

"I've forgotten something. I have to go back. You go ahead, I'll catch up with you."

Schascha ran.

And Carl walked on.

She rang the doorbell, and Mr. Darcy opened in surprise. "Has something happened?"

"Carl forgot to give you this book. It's his birthday today."

"In that case, shouldn't I be the one to give him a present?"

"It's a round-number birthday. Where he comes from, that's when you give other people gifts."

"Where does he come from?"

"Panama," said Schascha, who had read about the country in a book where the characters walked constantly. "Must go!"

Schascha caught up breathlessly with Carl, thinking how splendidly her plan had worked. And how good it was that her backpack now weighed a little less.

When they arrived at Effi's she was sitting by the window. It was the first time Carl had seen her there, her head sunk deep in the pages of her book. He was reminded of Darcy's wish, but it wouldn't have held true for Effi. There was no beauty in her reading. She held the heavy book like a shield in front of her face. Of course, anyone could simply tear a book away, but a person reading was in some special way protected, as if they were engaged in a sacred ritual.

The room behind Effi was dark. A shadow detached itself from the darkness and stepped toward her: a man, older than Effi, his white hair shaved close, his weathered features sharply defined, his build athletic. He looked like a soldier, and Carl shuddered to think how the name he had selected for Andrea Cremmen so closely suited her.

"Quick, ring the bell," he said to Schascha, who skipped immediately to press the button next to the gold nameplate.

Carl followed her, keeping a nervous eye on the window. He hoped Effi would get up, that the book lying in his backpack would offer her covering fire and open a path to the door. But her head sank deeper between the pages.

The door opened abruptly. Steel blue eyes stared down at him, a picture of reproach for the disturbance.

"Good evening, City Gate bookshop. I have a delivery for Mrs. Cremmen."

"Where do I sign?"

"I need a few words with Mrs. Cremmen about it."

"She's not at home."

Silence. Then Schascha piped up. "She's sitting by the window! I can see her. Right there." She pointed, as if her statement required evidence.

"She's not here. Come back tomorrow." The man slammed the door.

Effi glanced up, revealing her left cheek, red and swollen.

"Ring the bell again," commanded Schascha.

"No," replied Carl, "it might only make things worse for her."

"Or better!" Schascha rang the bell.

A shout came from inside, then Effi stood up. She opened the door a crack, just the width of a book, showing only the unbruised side of her face.

"I'm sorry, I'm not very well. I can't..."

"Did the man hit you?" asked Schascha. "Should we call the police?"

"No!" exclaimed Effi. "I must get back to him."

"Here's your book," said Carl. "We'll be back. Stay safe. Here's my number, if you want to talk to someone." He scribbled it quickly on a bookmark and passed it through the crack in the door. Then Effi's world closed once more.

Effi was alone again with her husband, Matthias, the man with whom she had fallen in love so deeply all those years ago. It had been during her time in the emergency department: Matthias had come in with minor injuries and small fractures. His body language shouted "coiled spring," his eyes clearly expert at spotting gaps in a person's defenses. Anyone could see there was something not quite right about this man in the perfectly fitting dark blue business suit. Effi could see it too—but she wanted to find out what it was. In treatment room 3, the man told her he'd been beaten up: three guys had laughed at him for reading a book on a park bench; he'd had no chance against them. That was the moment the seeds of Effi's love were planted. She'd chosen Matthias, believing a man who reads a book must have a sensitive heart. It didn't matter what else might be wrong with him—that would be enough to change him, to save him. She'd never asked which book he'd been reading. Its sensational title, printed in block capitals on the jacket, was *HOW TO WIN ANY BATTLE!* The three men had read it, taken it as provocation, and made derogatory remarks about Matthias. He'd leaped up in an instant and lashed out at them. He'd quickly lost the battle, but it had felt good. Later, he started going to the city's home soccer games at the weekend—not for the soccer, but for the postmatch fighting. Every punch he landed, every blow he felt, made him feel alive. The punches became addictive. At some point, he'd brought his addiction home to his own four walls. He still loved Effi, but he loved hitting her even more. Effi had never given up hope that the sensitive man with the book on the park bench would someday understand what was wrong with him. And she believed the more she loved and cared for him, the more beautiful she made their home, the sooner this would happen. But no matter how many things she did right, Matthias always found something wrong. And that was good enough grounds for a punch. He really didn't like hitting her, he said; it was just that she deserved it. Punishment was the only option, in his eyes. The tragedy was, Matthias honestly couldn't see any alternative.

It was no comfort to Carl that Effi had a new book to sustain her.

"That wasn't enough!" said Schascha. "We have to do more for her."

"You're right. We should think of a book that will help her."

Schascha had no answer to this, so she remained silent. As soon as they turned the corner, she realized she'd left something behind again. Carl wondered whether children were as forgetful as old people. He couldn't remember for certain.

When Schascha also forgot something at Mrs. Longstocking's (whose discovery of the day was "at the sight of her, he could barely contain his arbor"), Carl surreptitiously followed her back to the house. Dog appeared out of nowhere, accepted a small treat from Carl's old pastille tin, and they watched together as Schascha gave the old woman a book wrapped in candy-colored paper. After unfolding the paper, Mrs. Longstocking gave Schascha an affectionate hug, then disappeared momentarily, before returning to give Schascha a bar of chocolate.

Carl would have given a great deal to see the title on that book, but he didn't want to embarrass Schascha by interrupting them. He was sure an embarrassment-free opportunity would present itself shortly—if Schascha should happen to forget something at his final customer of the day.

She skipped up to Carl, took off her backpack, and swung it around her body like a dance partner. Dog looked on, disconcerted, with tail erect. Carl gave it an extra portion from the pastille tin as compensation. After all, these were strange times for Dog too.

The Reader was delighted with the new translation of Cervantes's *Don Quixote*.

"You read a lot," said Schascha.

"Eight hours every day at the factory, then more at home: I'm constantly on the lookout for new books to read to the women rolling the cigars."

"So you know a lot about books?"

"Ah, no matter how many books I read, there will always

be more that I haven't read. That's the tragedy. Anyone who enjoys reading wants to read every good book there is."

"If you can tell when a book is good, why don't you write one yourself?"

The Reader stared, dumbstruck.

Carl was surprised that Schascha hadn't asked *him* that question. Perhaps she thought a person who delivers books doesn't write any—much the same as parcel couriers don't create parcels, merely deliver them.

The Reader gave Carl a look. "You truly have a remarkable companion there."

"It wouldn't be the first time I've thought that," replied Carl. Frankly, he seemed to think it quite regularly.

"In fact, I have written a book. I've been working on it for ten years."

Dog wound its body around the Reader's legs, and Carl had the impression the cat was trying to calm the man; he seemed on edge.

"What's the book about?" asked Schascha. "You?"

The Reader smiled. "No, it's about a man who is deaf, who wants to learn the tango. But all the dance schools turn him away, so eventually he places an ad in the newspaper. He receives a reply from a woman who wants to teach him. She places the loudspeakers on the floor, and they dance barefoot, so he can feel the vibrations through the soles of his feet. They fall in love, but then the man discovers that his teacher is also deaf. He is devastated she has deceived him. He feels a deep sense of betrayal, because she can't hear the music either, and he turns his back on her."

"That's a dumb story," said Schascha. "Well, the ending is dumb. They should kiss."

"They do kiss, but by the end they don't."

"But that's the most important point! Kissing has to happen at the end. Before that, it doesn't count."

"You know," said the Reader, "life is often like that. Sometimes there is kissing, and sometimes the kissing stops. The only difference between a novel with a happy ending and one without is the point at which you cease telling the story."

"You don't understand what I mean. Nobody likes sad stories." As she said it, Schascha thought of Effi, and realized that was not entirely true. "Well, normal, happy people don't. Did many people buy your book?"

"No. No one has ever yet read it—I have never given it to anyone."

"You've not even read it out to anyone? At work? To your cigar ladies?"

"I wouldn't be able to get a single word out."

"Why not?"

"Because it might be really terrible."

"Give it to the Book Walker, he knows all about books." She pointed to Carl. "He'll tell you whether it's good or bad. But the ending is dumb, you know that now."

The Reader was as unmoving as a statue. Schascha feared he might never move again, but she guessed a great deal was running through his mind right at that moment.

"I couldn't possibly ask him to do that," he whispered to Schascha, although of course he knew Carl could hear.

"Course you could. He'd love to. He's nice. And he's always reading. So he could read your book too."

"Mr. Kollhoff, I'm sorry you've been put in such an embarrassing position. I would never expect such a favor from you. I'm certain you get requests like this all the time."

Such requests virtually never came Carl's way, and that was fine by him. If a manuscript was poor, how could he tell the client without hurting their feelings?

"You will do it, won't you?" asked Schascha. It was a rhetorical question.

Carl hesitated. He watched joy radiate from her pale blue eyes; he couldn't disappoint her. "Of course, I'd love to."

"I'll fetch it right away!" said the Reader, disappearing and returning with the manuscript in a shoebox. "And please, be honest—brutally honest. It's the only way I'll make progress." He gulped. Schascha couldn't even guess at what he might be swallowing, but it must have been something significant. "Take your time, read it at your leisure."

"It will be an honor and a privilege."

"That remains to be seen." The Reader gave an anxious smile. This was the moment he had both feared and yearned for in equal measure. Now his novel was out in the world. Admittedly, it had only taken one tiny step, with one single person, but his lines would finally fulfill the purpose for which they had been written: to gain a reader. He feared they might shatter in the process.

The Reader was at a loss for further words. "Then..."

"Bye!" said Schascha. "We've got work to do."

"Yes, of course, I mustn't keep you. See you soon. I've already placed my order for the next book by phone."

With their farewells taken, Schascha had once again forgotten something.

"I'll come with you," said Carl. "It's terribly boring waiting for you."

"It won't take long, you won't have time to be bored."

"I'll come anyway, the few extra steps will do me good." He watched with satisfaction as Schascha bit her lower lip, though guilt followed a moment later.

She slapped her forehead theatrically. "Oh no, I haven't forgotten anything. I'm such an idiot."

"Sure?"

"Positive!"

"Do you want to give him one of your books anyway?"

Schascha stamped her feet in fury. "Gaargh! You knew all along!"

"Only since Effi."

"You spied on me!"

"And you're working in competition with me."

"Am not. I'm not selling my books, I'm giving them away."

"Are they the books they should be reading?"

"Yes, they'll make them happy. You didn't want to do it, so I had to spend all the pocket money I'd saved up."

"So what were the books?"

"Mr. Darcy only reads stuff to *think* about, and I think it's time he *did* something—with his hands. So I gave him a book about woodworking; he's got a lot of wood in his garden."

"A natural choice. Mrs. Longstocking?"

"She loves finding mistakes. The more mistakes, the happier she is."

"I can't wait to find out what her book was…"

"I gave her one that shows two pictures side by side, but one of them has ten mistakes hidden in it. It's called—"

"Spot the Difference!" Admittedly, this wasn't quite the kind of mistake that old German teachers with failing eyesight would readily find. "I'm sure it'll keep her occupied for hours. Effi?"

"Something to make her laugh. *The Bumper Book of Silly Jokes.*"

Carl didn't believe for a minute that Effi would read more than a single page. But even if gifted books were never read, they were still a loving gesture—and a compliment to the intellect and taste of the recipient. Many an author's career has been founded on their books' gifting potential, rather than their content, provided the book served as an interior design statement, looked elegant on the bookshelf, and coordinated well with a gold-framed Dalí print of elephants on stilts.

"But I pushed the joke book through Effi's letter box. I didn't want to ring the bell again."

He looked toward the Reader's home. "What are you planning to give him?"

"That was so hard! I really didn't know what would make him happy. 'Cause I don't know what makes him unhappy."

"But you've brought a book for him?"

Schascha nodded, pulling a wrapped volume from her backpack. "It's by Alfred somebody; it's a book of new words."

"Alfred Heberth: *New Words. Neologisms in the German Language Since 1945*. A remarkable choice."

"I thought he's bound to enjoy reading words he's never heard of before. Like...*honeybeematador*."

"There is absolutely no such word."

"That's why it's so much fun to say. Ho-ney-bee-ma-ta-dor."

"What about *rootintootintinabulation*?"

She glanced sideways at him. "You can be funny sometimes!"

"Only by accident," replied Carl.

"You're not wrong. But it's not a bad thing."

"There's no way you found that book by yourself. Who recommended it to you?"

"The old man at the Moses secondhand bookshop. He's even older than you: his skin is as wrinkled as a raisin."

Hans was a wonderful and warmhearted man. Watching him work among books piled high on either side always put Carl in mind of a tortoise slowly stretching its neck out of its shell. Hans had inherited the business from his mother many years ago. Yet he himself never read books: his greatest act of filial rebellion had been a refusal to ever read Goethe, Schiller,

Fontane, Dürrenmatt or Tolstoy, in favor of the weekly comic book Western *Lassiter—Hardest Man of the Age*. Although he was familiar with the names of the most prominent authors and their works, and could even name the genres they wrote in, he hadn't read a single one. That role had been fulfilled by his wife, who had died at the beginning of the year. Now he was the proprietor of an antiquarian bookshop with no in-house reader.

"I told him I only had enough money for cheap books—just a few cents per book. But that wasn't a problem at all."

"And you found a book for each person?"

"Course. Well, the man found them. It was ever so easy. He had a box next to the till with all the right books."

The box was where Hans put all the volumes that would never sell. He gave them away to his best customers; it was a way to create space on the shelves. Carl was certain Hans hadn't found the right books in that box—or at most, only a couple of titles to fit the bill.

"Take the Reader his book; he'll be delighted."

"And what will you do?"

"I'll stay here and think."

"About what?" Schascha had learned it never boded well when adults "thought" yet did not reveal what they were thinking about.

"About how if I can't stop a bone-headed little girl's plan, then I should do whatever I can to make sure it goes as well as it possibly can."

"That's something you can think about for as long as you like!"

It was nine o'clock in the evening when Carl's phone rang—a sound he never entirely appreciated, being a quieter type. Carl jumped—both out of his skin, and out of Africa, where he had been rereading Karen Blixen's autobiography. He had last read it twenty-five years ago, and was in the habit of reopening each of his books every quarter century, to see whether they had anything new to tell him.

Carl tucked his current bookmark—an old till receipt from the bakery—between the pages and laid the book carefully to one side.

He smoothed his clothes, pulled his collar straight, and picked up the receiver.

"Kollhoff, good evening."

"Is that Carl Kollhoff?"

"Yes, speaking."

"This is the Münsterblick residential home. Gustav Gruber has asked to see you."

"But it's Saturday. He never wants visitors on a Saturday."

"He's not at all well. I think you'd best be quick."

Carl walked so quickly through the nighttime streets, he was completely out of breath by the time he arrived. On the way, he'd wondered whether to take Gustav something. But when a person is departing forever, they have to leave everything behind, even something they've only just received. Nonetheless, Carl bought a bunch of tulips in bright colors at the gas station. Gustav was fond of tulips: they reminded him of Amsterdam. The sight of them always cheered him. Of course, no one could take happiness with them either, but nor could anyone have too much happiness in life. Perhaps in a person's final moments it was more important than ever.

At the residential home, Carl didn't wait for the lift; he took the stairs. He gave a brief knock, and without waiting for a "come in," opened the door.

To be faced with Sabine Gruber.

Gustav lay in his bed, his breathing shallow and weak.

"You can't see him," said Sabine Gruber, putting her hand

against his chest and pushing him out. She wanted at least these few final moments alone with her father.

"No one can see him," she continued. "He needs peace and quiet." She closed the door behind her.

"How is Gustav?"

"I really don't have the time right now to talk to you about it."

"Is there anything I can do?"

"No, there's nothing you can do for him now."

"I mean for you. Can I bring you something to eat or drink? You look as though you could do with a little something."

"Mr. Kollhoff, I can manage perfectly well here without you." Without another word, she turned and left him.

Carl didn't want to leave his old boss alone. To walk out now would feel like turning his back on a drowning man.

He sat down, but immediately stood up again. Sitting felt like surrender. Instead, he began walking the corridors of the residential home, each as interchangeable, and as inescapable, as the tunnels of a labyrinth. The pervasive, vinegary smell of cleaning product hung everywhere.

As if from nowhere, a bookcase appeared in front of him. The home's library comprised a large number of well-thumbed volumes so worn they would not have found a buyer even at a flea market. It was a veritable literary hospice. Carl scanned the spines, the authors and titles. He wasn't sure at first what he was looking for, but the more he looked, the clearer it became in his mind.

He found *Emil and the Detectives* by Erich Kästner. Gustav must certainly have read it in his younger days.

Carl sat down with the book outside Gustav's room, and began to read.

The words wouldn't pass through the walls to Gustav, but Carl read aloud all the same. He knew the words possessed no magic to heal Gustav. He knew he was no Merlin, no Djedi, no Circe. Just Carl Kollhoff, whose voice cracked, and who missed his best friend.

He read the story of Emil Tischbein, and of Mr. Grundeis, who stole a hundred and forty deutsche marks from Emil on the train. He read about Gustav with his horn, about Pony with her bicycle, about the gang of young detectives and "Password *Emil*."

Carl didn't once glance at his wristwatch; he read without stopping, as though the thread of Gustav's life would slip away if the flow of words ceased.

Suddenly a nurse ran past him into Gustav's room, followed by several more in fluttering white aprons, like a flock of birds pursued by a hawk.

Carl read louder and faster, forcing the words out of the book, his fingers holding it so tightly they left indentations in the hard cover.

Then the flock of white birds swept out of the room again, slowly now, with heads bowed.

Once they had all left the room, Carl slowly closed the book, laid it gently on the floor next to Gustav's door, and left the building. In his eyes, it was uninhabited now.

The old copper bell that announced the arrival of a customer at the City Gate bookshop always rang out a cheery major chord, but when Carl entered the building the following day, it sounded in his ears in a minor key.

An easel had been set up at the entrance, supporting a large, framed photo draped in black crepe. It showed Gustav being presented with his retirement gifts by Sabine. He could barely be seen behind the enormous bouquet, and his smile was no more than a pale echo of his daughter's radiant, beaming face.

Even then, Gustav had no longer been himself; his transformation into a shadow had already begun.

In front of the easel stood a small table draped in a pristine white jacquard cloth, on which lay a book of condolence. Carl leafed through the heavy pages with trembling fingers. There were drawings of hearts, words of mourning and loss. Many customers had shared memories of Gustav, or mentioned books he had recommended, and what these meant for them.

A matte black calligraphy pen lay beside it in wordless challenge.

Carl could always sense appropriate words when he read them, but he was never good at finding suitable words to write himself. And they had to be the right words for Gustav. Writing the wrong words in memoriam of a man of words would be like offering a chef a lamentably bad rendition of his own signature dish.

Behind the desk, staring at the computer screen as she typed, her hair falling over her face, stood Sabine Gruber in a black sheath dress.

Carl stepped toward her. "My deepest condolences for… your loss." Using the formal *Sie* felt stranger than ever on his lips.

"Thank you," replied Sabine Gruber, without looking up. "We need to talk."

"Whenever you need a listening ear, I'm here for you, Sabine. Or a shoulder, you know."

This time, she looked up, but not into his eyes; she seemed to be focusing on a point in the middle of Carl's forehead. "*Mr.* Kollhoff, it's not about my father, it's about the bookshop."

Carl's world was so filled with grief, there was no room left to notice the sharp undertone in her voice. "Of course, I'm always here to help you with the bookshop too."

"While my father was still alive, there were many things

I couldn't put into action, because it would have upset him. I'm sure you understand that I don't wish to lose any more time in implementing the changes vital to the survival of our bookshop."

The sentence sounded like one she had written down in advance and practiced multiple times.

"Yes, of course," said Carl, who still had no inkling of where this conversation was leading.

"We're discontinuing your delivery service. In future, book orders placed with us can be collected here, or dispatched from our wholesaler. Please inform the customers on your final round today. If there is anyone you are not able to speak to today, that person will receive a communication from us."

"Is this because of my fee? I'll stop taking the money."

"Mr. Kollhoff, it's not just the money. I have already explained to you in great detail the additional effort."

"But the customers give most of their orders to me personally, and I enter them into the system."

"I really don't wish to discuss the store's internal processes with you right now. This is my bookshop, and my decision." She continued typing on the keyboard. "It's purely a business decision, and an entirely rational one. Please don't make this a bigger issue than it is. You can use your free evenings for something more enjoyable."

It took all of Carl's effort just to stand. For the first few moments, he couldn't even think. Only when he realized he'd forgotten to breathe did he begin thinking again—and filling his lungs with air. Use his free evenings for something more enjoyable? There was nothing more enjoyable for him than taking books to other people!

"I'll buy the books here, like a normal customer, and deliver them. Then it's no more effort for you."

"In which case, our insurance wouldn't cover you for the delivery."

"That's my own risk."

"Mr. Kollhoff, this is exactly the kind of discussion I wished to avoid."

"But—"

"It would still appear to be an official service provided by our bookshop. If there were to be any misconduct toward the customers, it would reflect badly on us. Now, I really have better things to do than continue this discussion. Could everyone please get back to work!"

Carl hadn't noticed the bookshop's three employees, plus Leon, the work experience student, gathering to his right and left.

"Mr. Kollhoff has never acted with any misconduct toward a customer," said Vanessa Eichendorff. Carl had shown her the ropes many years ago, encouraging her to get through that difficult initial period and not give up.

"There's never been a single complaint," added Julia Berner, to whom Carl had once given thirty deutsche marks to make the till balance when she'd made a mistake cashing up on her first day.

"The only thing that Carl's behavior reflects on us is how much care we take of our customers." This came from Jochen Giesing, whose daughter Lily had once gained a student traineeship at the bakery where Carl bought his croissants every morning, thanks to Carl putting in a good word. Carl regarded the baker as his friend, on the grounds that he had been a customer there for twenty-seven years, and the exchange of fresh-baked goods for shining coinage gave them a special sort of connection.

Leon felt obliged to say something. "Because of Mr. Kollhoff, my whole family have been buying their books here for years. Even all the ones I never read!"

Sabine Gruber's pupils twitched nervously; the pulse in her neck throbbed nervously; her hands nervously moved a pen from left—where it had lain quite conveniently—to right. Today was the day Sabine Gruber wanted to draw a line under the past. She had already removed everything from the office that reminded her of her father: a photo of Gustav with the young man from Behlendorf who had gone on to be a Nobel Prize winner; Gustav's City Culture Award certificate, given to him as thanks for the many literary events he had organized; even the clumsy picture of him that Sabine had drawn in kindergarten. She didn't want any reminders of him: it was too painful. The biggest reminder of all was Carl Kollhoff, to whom her father would certainly have left the bookshop, had tradition not dictated otherwise.

Looking into the eyes of all her employees, Sabine Gruber realized they were not prepared to let her father go, and that for them too, Carl Kollhoff was the final remaining connection.

It appeared today was not the day to cut that final cord.

But it was the day to make clear to everyone that the scissors lay ready.

"We'll discuss this another time," she said. It was a threat no one could misunderstand.

Carl wrapped his books in silence. The action of folding the edges of the paper, the soft tearing of sticky tape, the rasping sound of one paper packet rubbing against another in his backpack, the whole familiar routine calmed his breathing but not his heart. He was on probation: a single mistake would lead to exile. Carl also wrapped the books he'd chosen as gifts for his customers, to make them happy, just as Schascha had planned.

Which book would he choose for himself, if he was dismissed? Sabine Gruber's computer would undoubtedly recommend a book of practical activities for a man of his age. Raised-bed gardening, cooking with two ingredients, crocheting beanie hats, silk painting, perhaps a study program for senior citizens. Any of those could make a person happy, provided the person hadn't just lost the one activity that had made him happy for decades. They would be no more than a substitute, as bitter tasting as chicory coffee to someone accustomed to fresh, ground beans.

Even the sight of Schascha in her yellow winter coat, looking like a sun on two legs under the overcast sky, did nothing to lighten his mood.

"You look different," she said by way of greeting.

"I'm still the same person."

"Your eyes are different." Schascha took a step back to scrutinize them.

"I only have the one pair; they're not something anyone can change."

"Have you been crying?"

"No."

"Have you been crying on the inside maybe? Not with tears in your eyes, but like, with your heart?"

"With tears in my heart?"

"If that's a thing, then yes."

"In that case, why would my eyes look different?"

"They're ashamed, because crying should be their job."

Carl stroked a fingertip over his eyelids, in case his eyes really were ashamed, and needed a little care.

"Can I ask something else?" asked Schascha.

"You don't usually seek permission. Normally you just ask."

"I'm a bit worried you'll think it's a silly question."

"That's never bothered you before, and I see no reason to change things. Out with it."

"Have you got a name for me today?"

"No. I can't think of any book character who's like you."

"But I want one! You'll have to read more books!"

"I expect I'll be doing just that very soon," said Carl, though he didn't explain why.

Dog appeared, earlier than usual, and began rubbing its flank against Carl's right leg, where the pastille tin of treats was kept. Carl gave it nothing. *Will it still come back?* he wondered. As he bent down to stroke its head, it dodged away. Clutching at air, Carl stumbled headlong. Cobblestones are notoriously hard, and these had a centuries-old history of defiance, yielding neither to horse-drawn carriages nor to tank tracks. Carl touched down on his knees, then fell sideways. Pain shot through all his limbs, but the disappointment smarted more. He'd never fallen over on his round, never had so much as a momentary slip. He'd always been able to rely on his stout shoes, thick socks, and his feet. It seemed the world was changing, and not just in a single aspect: the changes were ambushing him like a pack of hungry wolves surrounding an injured sheep.

"Here, let me help you," said Schascha, holding out her hand. Carl took it, but supported himself on the cobbles, not wanting to pull on her hand in case she lost her balance. "Shall I carry your backpack today? I can manage two."

"No," said Carl, standing up. His knees were throbbing, and the palms of his hands were grazed. "It would feel wrong to do my round with no weight on my back."

The backpack had slipped off as he fell, and Schascha handed it back to him. "It's really heavy. Have you only got the books you like in there? Or are you delivering others as well?"

"I like your questions." Carl brushed the dirt from his clothes. "But I can't cope with so many today. I don't have the energy for them."

"That's not an answer!"

He sighed. "I'm also delivering books I don't like, or ones that don't speak to me. You know, no book speaks to everyone. And even a foolish book can provoke intelligent thinking. A little bit of stupidity never did anyone any harm. You just have to take care it doesn't get out of hand and spread." It was a rare thing for Carl to lie, telling a customer that a book was out of print, and he always felt guilty when he did. He'd once refused to bring one to Effi, because he'd heard that a woman had sunk into depression after reading it.

"I've got another question."

"Another time. I don't want to talk today."

"Just one more! Pleasepleaseplease!"

"Why can't you ever let it go?"

Schascha took that as a yes, although she would have asked her question even if it had been a no. She had a feeling Carl would sink deeper into melancholy if they didn't talk to one another. Her questions were life preservers for his thoughts, keeping them with her on the surface.

"Have you ever not taken on a customer? Or canceled one?"

Carl was so irritated, he forgot his sadness for a moment. "Yes, out of self-defense. Just as I'm shutting up right now out of self-defense!"

"Was it Effi's husband? Did he hit you?"

"What? No! Where's Dog?"

The cat had walked away without a sound.

"Why then?" asked Schascha. "Tell me!"

Carl sighed. He was really in no mood to give an answer, but he had even less desire to lose his second companion. Being alone would be even worse than Schascha's questions.

"It was a woman who always broke the spine. The first thing she did with a new book was bend the covers back until it cracked."

"Grim!" It occurred to Schascha that this was a cue to spit on the ground in contempt, but disgust got the better of her.

"She said it made them easier to hold in one hand, and they wouldn't fall shut so easily. She used to do it as soon as she'd unwrapped them; she could hardly wait. In the end, I couldn't bear the sound. Happy now?"

Schascha thought about the books in her backpack. "I think you did the right thing. Can I buy you an ice cream?"

"Because I answered your question?"

"No, because ice cream always cheers people up."

"Not with all problems. Certainly not with mine."

"You're wrong. It works on anything. That's the great thing about ice cream."

At Pino's, she insisted Carl had an ice cream called the Penguin, which had hazelnut chocolate cream swirled through it. It was astonishingly sweet, intensified further by Schascha's choice of sugar strand topping.

She was right: the ice cream did help, and when two drops of it dripped onto Carl's right boot, making it look like it had eyes, and a slightly crazy expression, they both laughed.

That evening, Carl told all his customers they should order from him personally from now on—preferably when he called, but if not, by phone. He could be contacted at almost any time. Otherwise the risk was too great that Sabine Gruber would persuade them to stop using Carl's services. If that happened, there would be no one to object to his dismissal. No customers, no Carl.

Schascha had only brought books for those people to whom she had not yet given anything. Doctor Faustus found himself the owner of a *World's Cutest Puppies* calendar, a gift he did his very best to look pleased about. For Mr. Darcy, Carl had brought a collectors' edition of *Pride and Prejudice*, calling it a small token of the bookshop's gratitude for his years of loyalty. Darcy protested he had only yesterday received a book to celebrate Carl's Panamanian birthday, and that woodworking was much more fascinating than he had ever imagined. He peeked from the corner of his eye at Schascha, who immediately grew three centimeters taller.

Although Effi had not placed an order that day, they passed by her house, to see how she was. The windows were dark, and no one opened the door when they rang. Carl dropped *Dr. Erich Kästner's Lyrical Home Pharmacy* into her letter box, on the grounds that she needed help in many areas of her life, although he wasn't at all sure whether Kästner's ingenious rhymes would suffice.

Sitting at Hercules's kitchen table, Schascha asked how he had enjoyed the *Werther* (the title had been easy enough to remember).

"Do you know, it's an epistolary novel, in which the young Werther, a law student, is hopelessly in love with Lotte, who is engaged to another man." Schascha was taken aback: those were the exact words Carl had used to describe the book. Hercules might as well have learned them by heart.

The book (red binding) Carl had chosen for him was a volume summarizing all the most significant works of world literature. Hercules didn't seem at all pleased as he unwrapped it. The look of puzzlement on his face gave way to a halfhearted smile as Schascha explained the reasoning behind Carl's gift.

"Now you don't need me to summarize the novels for you," said Carl. "You have genuine experts in this book."

Like a light switching off, the halfhearted smile disappeared again.

It was Schascha who understood. Leaning across to Carl, she whispered, "Watch his eyes!"

Then she opened the book and turned to Hercules. She drew the tip of her finger down the table of contents. "These are the titles of all the greatest novels. Here's *Rügen Island*. That's a really famous one, have you read it?"

"No, not yet."

"But you must have read this one?" She tapped a title, and left her question hanging in the air for a moment. *"The Stein Family Sheep."*

"Sadly, not that one either. But you must carry on telling me about the novels, Mr. Kollhoff! I'm sure this book is great, but the stories really come alive when you tell them."

"Of course, if you wish, I would love to continue."

The light came on again. Hercules wanted to hear the plots of *Rügen Island* and *The Stein Family Sheep* in great detail, and Carl told the stories as best he could, under the circumstances. It was a fine achievement, given he had never read either of the books, since they didn't exist.

As they stepped back onto the street, Carl took a deep breath. "He can't read a word."

"Poor man."

"Why Rügen, sheep and Stein?"

"I went there last year on holiday with my dad. We stayed with the Steins. They have loads of sheep—they're so cute! It was the best I could think of in a hurry. Please can we help Hercules?"

"I think we have to!"

"But a book won't help."

"No. And whatever we do to help him, he mustn't feel embarrassed. Because he does at the moment, very much."

"Feeling embarrassed sucks. I know—I get embarrassed all the time."

They continued in silence.

At some point, the effects of the Penguin ice cream began to wear off. There are days when a person needs more of it than they can eat.

On their way home, they passed by the Reader's home, although they had nothing in their backpacks for him that day.

"What's his book like?" asked Schascha. "Can you write a happy ending for it?"

He hadn't yet read a single word. He knew he couldn't put it off any longer.

Carl pulled the big wing chair away from the French window. He didn't want to watch the city today, didn't want to look out for his customers in the streets and alleyways, nor for Dog on the roof ridges and terraces. There was too much pain and anxiety out there.

In preparation for reading, he'd brewed a large pot of herbal tea, which now sat over a tea light on a warming stand to keep to temperature.

Carl divided readers into hares, tortoises, and fish. He himself was a fish, allowing a book to carry him in its current, as its pace moved between fast and leisurely. Hares were speed-readers, hurtling through a book and promptly forgetting what they had read just a few pages earlier, forever needing to flip the pages back to check. Tortoises flipped back too, because they read so slowly that months passed before they finished a book. Every evening they would read a single page, then fall asleep. Sometimes, they would read the same page again the next night, because they weren't sure how far they'd got. Each of these animals could, at a moment's notice, transform into a curious lapwing, leaping to the back of the book to see the ending first, before reading the rest. To Carl's way of thinking, that was like going to a restaurant and eating dessert first.

Of course it was sweet and delicious, but the anticipation fueled by the preceding savory courses was lost.

Regardless of which animal a reader was, opening a new book was always a significant moment. It made Carl uneasy each time. Would it live up to the expectations generated by title, cover, and blurb? Would it perhaps even exceed them? Would the language and style succeed in moving him?

He had barely read the first sentence before he could hear the Reader's warm baritone. The entire novel seemed to consist of words demanding to be spoken aloud. Anatomically impossible though it was, every line seemed to have been written with the ears. Of course it contained brutal words too, but even in those passages, the Reader had chosen words with a sound that was pleasing to the ear. Carl automatically began to read the book aloud, something he never usually did.

He did not once reach for the tea.

Carl found he was in fact reading two books at the same time. The deaf man, who was so eager to learn tango, was also secretly writing a novel. It told the tale of a hot-air balloon pilot who built himself an airship so large, with such a vast gondola, that it could contain all of life's necessities, removing the need to ever set foot on the ground again.

When the deaf man broke off his relationship with the dance teacher, because she had been deceiving him all the while, he at least allowed his pilot the happiness of landing to find the love of his life, giving the couple a life of both literal and metaphorical down-to-earth bliss together.

Perhaps Schascha would accept one happy ending out of two.

Carl smiled as he thought of her. He missed her—even more so than the delivery service.

As he reached the end of the manuscript, Carl felt simultaneously very happy, and a little melancholy. Even when an extraordinary book ends at precisely the right point, with precisely the right words, and anything further would only destroy that perfection, it still leaves us wanting more pages. That is the paradox of reading.

Carl would tell the Reader how much the book had moved him. But he very much doubted his opinion would suffice.

The Reader would have to experience for himself just how good his book was.

And Carl had an idea how to achieve exactly that.

chapter 5

Words

IT OFTEN SURPRISED CARL how the weather in novels reflected the mood of the protagonist. The weather in his city was perfectly indifferent to his mood. While he felt full of purpose, the sky had clothed itself in a dirty gray, and the few drops falling from the swollen clouds were doing so with pinpoint accuracy. He turned up his jacket collar: there wasn't quite enough rain for his umbrella. A few more drops, and he could have justified opening it. This was nothing less than a devious quantity of rain.

It matched Schascha's mood perfectly.

She had pulled her hat with the fake pilot's goggles low over her forehead. Today, Schascha was a sad sun.

"What's wrong?"

"That idiot Simon!" It had all the vehemence of a potent curse.

"Penguin ice cream?" asked Carl—after all, Schascha herself had said it always improved a person's mood.

"Nah," replied Schascha truculently.

"Two scoops with sprinkles?"

"Okay," said Schascha without hesitation. "But it has to be right now."

And so it was that, for the first time ever, Carl altered the route of his book round.

Pino's little ice cream parlor was offering chocolate sauce or sprinkles that day. Schascha wanted both. Carl had one scoop—it would have been rude to let Schascha eat alone.

It's impossible to slurp ice cream with a stern expression, and their faces soon relaxed.

"What did Simon do?"

She licked at some ice cream that was threatening to dribble down the cone. "Came over to me at break time and pushed me. Just like that. Right into a bush! I scratched my arm." She showed it to him. "There! It bled too!" Schascha knew that the laurel hedge had only inflicted three tiny scratches. She also knew it had only been a light nudge, and she had fallen badly due to her heavily loaded schoolbag. She even knew that Simon had run away mortified afterward. But when a drama occurs in life, it's only reasonable to overdramatize the retelling a little for effect.

"It must hurt," said Carl.

"Too right!"

"Does it need to be kissed better?"

"Pfff! As if that would help! This is a *real* wound!"

The healing powers of a kiss seemed to have vanished along with Santa Claus and the Easter Bunny.

"I think your Simon likes you."

"Because he pushes me?" Schascha licked at her ice cream with greater ferocity—her way of indicating her annoyance at this speculation.

"That's what boys do. At that age, they don't know how to talk to girls."

"But they know how to push us!"

"Exactly. There's even a specialist term for it: negative contact. See, there's scientific evidence."

"Simon's still an idiot!" She bit the cornet until it cracked.

Carl understood that at Schascha's age, *idiot* and *boy* were synonyms as far as girls were concerned. Agreement seemed appropriate. "All boys are young idiots, until they become men." He glossed over the unfortunate possibility that they might then become adult idiots.

"Should we go find Simon and push him?" he asked.

Schascha stared at him in disbelief. Then she laughed out loud, spraying cornet crumbs into the air. It took her some time to get her breath back. "Nah, I'm not as big an idiot as him. It's time to deliver books!"

Schascha complained about Simon the whole way to Sister Amaryllis, with new irritations constantly springing to mind as they walked. Simon had painted a stupid smiley on her pencil case, hidden her schoolbag (next to his!), and picked her to be on his team for sports, even though she was lousy at dodgeball. He really had it in for her! What had she ever done to him? At kindergarten they'd played so nicely at happy families together, either with a cuddly lion as their child, or Annette with the big ears.

The nun had ordered yet another thriller with blood oozing from every page. Carl added his gift of a legal textbook on the subject of housing rights. Perhaps it would contain a clause that enabled her to stay in her convent. And in case it didn't, he'd brought flour and candles as well.

Their next stop was Mrs. Longstocking, who came straight to the door.

"It's you! Just a second!" She disappeared momentarily.

When she returned, not only had she tied back her disheveled hair, but she was also proudly holding *Spot the Difference!*

"I found them all!" She opened the book and showed them the places, ringed in red pen. "There were even additional mistakes in the short accompanying texts. Maybe I get extra points for those." She gave a smile of satisfaction. "Thank you again. I haven't had such fun in a long time. You know, I miss my students so much. Especially the ones who struggled. They were the ones I could teach the most to."

The idea had been waiting in the wings of Carl's mind for some time. Now was its moment to step into the spotlight.

He turned to Schascha. "Would you do me a favor?"

"Course."

"Without getting an ice cream in return?"

"Already had one." She grinned. "But I'd eat another one, if that did you a favor!"

"Scoot over to Hercules and see if he's in. If you can, make sure he stays there. No going shopping or out to bodybuilding. Then run back and let me know. Hurry!"

Schascha nodded and ran off, while Mrs. Longstocking presented Carl with "fartified wine"—her typo of the day. It felt good to run for something important—it made her feet run faster, her heart beat faster, and best of all, was an excuse to shout "Out of the way!" Unfortunately, it wasn't far to Hercules's apartment block. Without pausing to think, she rang the bell.

"Hello? Who's there?" called the intercom.

"It's Schascha, from the Book Walker—I mean, from Mr. Kollhoff."

"But I haven't ordered anything."

"Are you home? I mean, will you be staying home?"

"Erm, yes, why?"

"No bodybuilding studio or shopping?"

"Schascha?"

"Yes?"

"Why are you asking such odd questions?"

"Just say yes or no! But preferably yes!"

"I'm not going anywhere else today."

"Awesome. Thanks, Hercules!"

"Hercu...who?"

Schascha was already gone. When she arrived back, Mrs. Longstocking was already putting on a coat. In her agitation, her hand missed the sleeve several times.

"It isn't far," said Carl by way of encouragement. He had already discussed the details with her. "If this works, I'm sure he could come to you in future." He opened his umbrella. "This will make it feel less difficult, won't it?"

Mrs. Longstocking looked up into the vast sky, stretching endlessly above her. Her sight clouded, but she could feel Carl's hand on her upper arm, supporting her. She hadn't been outside for so long, she felt like an infant taking its first faltering steps. When *was* the last time she'd left the house? It had never been her plan to avoid the open sky forever. But days had become weeks, then months, then years. The more time that passed, the greater the fear grew of leaving her safe retreat where walls and ceilings protected her from the outside world.

But now a new student needed her. Carl Kollhoff had made it quite plain that she was his only hope.

In all her lifetime, there would never be a better reason to step outside.

The trembling in her knees slowly calmed, though it did not disappear altogether. Carl's firm grip gave Mrs. Longstocking a sense of security, and the child hopping to and fro in front of her took away some of the fear. After a short way, they were joined by a cat, which emitted a noise very like a bark. She must have misheard.

Schascha rang Hercules's doorbell again.

"Hello? Who's there?" called the intercom.

"It's Schascha again, but I've got Mr. Kollhoff with me this time."

"But I still haven't ordered a book," laughed Hercules.

Carl leaned forward. "It's about something else. I need to ask you a favor."

Buzzing. "Come on up then."

Hercules was already standing in the stairwell when they arrived on his floor.

"Thank you for making the time for us," said Carl.

"For you, anytime, no problem."

"This is Mrs.—" Dammit! Carl had thought of her as Mrs. Longstocking for so long, he had completely blanked out her real name, despite seeing it next to her doorbell each time. Like a blind spot.

"Dorothea Hillesheim, pleased to meet you," said Mrs. Longstocking. "But some of my friends call me Mrs. Longstocking." She threw Carl a look, who threw it on to Schascha, who threw it to the ground, where no one could see it.

They went into the kitchen, where Hercules offered them a drink.

"So, how can I help you?" asked Hercules, sitting down beside them with their drinks.

"I'm an elementary schoolteacher," began Mrs. Longstocking.

Hercules drew his eyebrows together like a boxer anticipating a mighty punch.

"And one of my students is illiterate. He can't read or write."

He cleared his throat. "I'm not sure how I can help you with that. I work at a builder's yard."

"The problem is, he doesn't respect me. I've developed an outstanding method of teaching him to read and write, but

I'm an old woman. Young at heart, naturally, but he thinks I'm…uncool. I need someone cool, someone he'd respect. He's a massive fan of some green action hero with muscles the size of hams, absolutely idolizes him. I told Mr. Kollhoff about my problem, and he had the idea of asking you to help me."

"Um, that's…"

"Of course, I'd have to teach you my system first, so that you can pass the teaching on to him. I wouldn't throw you in at the deep end! It's quite labor-intensive, I don't want you to be under any illusion. We'd have to work through every letter, because I've developed special catchphrases for each one." Mrs. Longstocking looked up at Hercules, who was massaging his knuckles. "I would completely understand it if you were to decline. I realize this has come as a surprise, and I'm sure you have many other demands on your time. It's just this student, you know? I like him a lot, he's a really good boy. But no one has ever properly taught him to read and write, and I don't want that to hold him back in life." Mrs. Longstocking took a sip of her mineral water, fervently hoping she hadn't laid it on too thick, or too transparently.

"You could have a superhero costume made," suggested Schascha. "You could be Captain Alphabet, or ABC-Man. I'd want to learn with you!"

Hercules took a deep breath. "Well, I have to say…" Another deep breath. "That's an awesome idea! What kind of an asshole would I be to say no?" He held out a paw. "I'm in! But I'll have to ask loads of questions, to make sure I really understand it all. Teach it to me like I'm that boy. If I do a thing, I do it a hundred percent. I think it's a great idea to help kids with their ABCs!"

Carl had to fight back a beaming smile. Schascha spared herself the struggle, and Mrs. Longstocking shook Hercules's hand for so long, it looked like she was doing a workout.

The Book Walker leaned slowly down toward Schascha. "Tomorrow morning, I'll need your help again. Can you ask your father if you're allowed to come?"

"Course I'm allowed. He always leaves the house before me anyway—he doesn't mind."

"You might be a bit late for school, but it's the only way."

"My first two lessons tomorrow are only sports. Simon would just push me again."

"It won't take long. But just in case you want to be a professional sportswoman when you grow up, you shouldn't skip your sports classes."

"Nah, not me."

Hercules fetched a schnapps to toast their joint project with Mrs. Longstocking, and the two of them continued talking, barely pausing for breath.

Carl bent down to Schascha again. "So what *do* you want to be when you grow up?"

"Don't know."

"I wanted to be mayor."

"Nah, I'm no good at organizing anything. Last year, we put on a fete for the animal rescue center, and everyone had to have a stand. I did lemonade. Made with real lemons! I had a table, a plastic tablecloth, loads of glasses—lemons, of course. All that. I was the only one where nothing went right, and everyone made fun of me. I'm never organizing anything ever again! Never in my whole life!"

"But you organized the books for my customers."

"That was one book for each of them. And I got them all from the secondhand bookseller. That wasn't real organizing. I want a job where other people do the organizing. I want to be an employee, like you."

"But an employee where?"

"Don't care, just an employee. Somewhere without lemons."

★ ★ ★

Carl was awake before the alarm. He checked the clock face again: this hadn't happened to him for ages. A good half hour early. Instead of turning over, he sprang out of bed with a sprightly leap—at least, for a man of his age and condition—and began making preparations for a red-letter day. Chief among these was conquering his own nervousness.

The previous day, he had phoned the Torcedor cigar factory in Bechtelstrasse pretending to be an editor at the city's newspaper, conducting research on their Reader for an article. It had taken a half bottle of Franconian Silvaner to summon the Dutch courage for the call. His speech had been a little slurred as a result, but the factory owner had shown no surprise. Perhaps she considered a certain blood-alcohol level completely normal in journalists. Carl had inquired when the factory opened, what time the Reader arrived, and whether he brought his books with him, or whether they were kept on-site. The latter, he was told. The book he read from was always left on a lectern. The workers started at eight o'clock, the Reader a half hour later.

It suited Carl's plan perfectly.

Carl stared at his breakfast several times, as though someone had exchanged it for something new. It was the same amount of butter spread on the same Paderborn loaf, topped with the same medium-mature Gouda that he always bought, but it tasted different, as did his cup of Feinste Milde ground coffee—a blend he had not changed since it first came on the market. Carl couldn't remember it ever tasting so good, or so rich, before. And his breakfast tasted so powerfully of cheese, butter, and bread, it felt as if he was appreciating the individual components for the very first time. He even dared to make himself a second slice, which was tantamount to gluttony.

As he took his coat from the hook, his gaze fell on the pile of books on the hall stand, waiting to be taken back to the library. A stack of children's books he had been scouring in search of Schascha. She wanted a name so badly, but he simply couldn't find one. None of the girls in the books was like her. Perhaps it was too late for a name; perhaps he knew her too well already. A name from a book was always like a corset, and once a personality was properly developed, it would burst out. No one would put a butterfly back in its cocoon. Nonetheless, he would continue his search for the girl who now accompanied him every day.

As he set foot on the pavement in front of his building, Carl couldn't help thinking of Mrs. Longstocking, who only the previous day had stepped into a world that had become entirely foreign to her. He felt exactly the same. This was his city, and he knew every cobblestone in the two square kilometers of its center. And yet it was not his city, but some other variant of it. He never entered it before nine o'clock in the morning, and never stayed in it beyond nine o'clock at night. Carl had no idea what happened here at other times: the people moving through its streets, their voices, and the sounds of other times of day, were all strange to him.

Walking to the cigar factory, he saw his city with fresh eyes.

Two hundred meters from his destination, he stopped at the lights on the busy four-lane road that marked the boundary of his world. He didn't press the button, but stood staring across the invisible border to the factory beyond.

Schascha was standing there, waving at him. It was a continuous wave, as if she was reeling in a line that drew him toward her. After three phases of the lights, he finally pressed the button, and walked through the invisible wall to the factory.

He left his small island, because a part of that island had detached itself from the mainland.

Schascha was restlessly shifting her weight from one foot

to the other. "Are you going to tell me now why we've come here?"

"You're the key," said Carl.

"What does that mean?"

"From now on, you're the Reader's niece, who wants to organize a surprise for him."

"Why aren't you his uncle?"

"Because no one can refuse a cute little girl like you. A weird old man is another matter."

"I'm not little!"

Carl looked around to check if anyone was listening. He even checked for open windows in the factory before continuing. "Tell them your uncle has written a book for the factory workers, but doesn't have the courage to read it to them. It's a marvelous book. Your plan is to put it on the lectern, and take away the book that's there, so he has no choice but to read it aloud. That's mostly the truth."

"Apart from the bit that's a lie."

"Sometimes I wish you were younger and more easily influenced."

"I'll do it. But in my own way."

"Oh, I don't know whether—"

"I'll tell them that in my family we celebrate Uncles' Day, when we all do something special for our uncles."

"That's...actually, that's even better."

Schascha, too, had stepped into a whole new world today. She had never even heard of places like this, where everything revolved around smoking. In the entrance, humidors of every shape and size stood next to dark wing chairs. Instead of the glittering jewelry they might be expected to contain, they were all filled with strange, unappetizing sausages. There were also glass cabinets of exquisite cigar cutters and sparkling lighters. The space smelled earthy and spicy, and was sparsely lit, with light filtering in fine stripes through slatted shutters. She could hear music playing in a foreign language. She felt Carl nudge her gently forward; her astonishment had brought her to a standstill.

A dark-haired woman appeared. When she spoke, her words appeared to contain far more *r*'s than was actually possible. Mercedes Riemenschneider was half Cuban, half German, and the owner of a factory that was half dream, half nightmare. Many people these days were rejecting the pleasures of mild intoxication in favor of healthy living. Mercedes Riemenschneider took the opposite view: pleasure played a leading role in her life. She also firmly believed that this should be obvious to others, and that wearing tight-fitting, low-cut dresses should not be the sole preserve of whip-thin women.

Schascha offered up her story, although she was unable to look the proprietor in the eye, staring fixedly instead at the wooden floorboards.

When she was finished, Mercedes Riemenschneider stroked Schascha's dark curls. "What a wonderful idea! Come with me!" She took a few steps, then turned. "Shouldn't you be at school?"

"We've got the first two classes free today, because Mrs. Brückner's ill. I think she's pregnant." Details, Schascha knew, were what made a lie credible.

Mercedes Riemenschneider drew a heavy burgundy curtain to one side, revealing a hall with twenty tables. The women sitting at them looked up, smiling. Each of them had a wooden board, on which the cigars were rolled, as well as a cardboard box full of tobacco leaves. There were chopping knives, small scissors, grooved trays for the finished cigars, and a number of other tools, but the most important of all was their hands. They had to be soft and elastic, and the cigar rollers had to have dexterity and a good eye. Cigars have to be rolled with exactly the right firmness to enable the smoke to find its way through the leaves.

At the end of the hall stood the lectern with the Reader's current book. Schascha sidled up to it and surreptitiously stashed the copy of *Robinson Crusoe* in her backpack, then laid the unpublished manuscript on the lectern.

"Let's go," said Carl.

"But I want to wait until he reads it!"

"No, you really must get to school now."

Mercedes Riemenschneider stepped next to Carl. "I thought the child had her first two classes free?"

Carl smiled, his lips tight. "Yes, but it's quite a long way. And I'm not so steady on my feet anymore."

The factory owner stepped behind them and laid her hands on Schascha's shoulders. "Give your granddaughter the pleasure of seeing him. He'll be here any moment. You can hide by the rear exit, he won't see you there."

As soon as they were standing unseen in the shadows, the Reader entered, shaking the hand of everyone in the room, but not speaking a word. He wore a red scarf around his neck, and was, on the whole, dressed too warmly for the time of year. He seemed determined to convince any potential virus particles from afar that any attempted assault on their part was doomed to failure.

"He's going to the desk," whispered Schascha, barely able to contain her excitement.

"Shh!" said Carl, who felt exactly the same, but didn't want to show it.

The Reader approached the lectern. Seeing the manuscript lying there, he paused. He looked around, searching for Carl, the one and only person to whom he had given it. But Carl was nowhere to be seen. He turned back to the lectern, picked up the manuscript, checked underneath it, then cast around on the floor, looking for *Robinson Crusoe*. But the book had abandoned its post, unlikely as that seemed.

The proprietor of the cigar factory approached him. "Is everything all right?"

"My book is gone. Has someone been here and taken it away?" He asked the question again, this time addressing the employees. "Does anyone have my book?"

Everyone looked at Mercedes Riemenschneider, who gave an imperceptible shake of the head. "There's something on your desk. Is that not yours?"

"No—I mean, yes, but…"

"Just read what's there. Everyone's waiting. You could read the telephone book and everyone would hang on your every word, your voice is so beautiful." The factory owner had a weakness for the Reader, and an even greater weakness for his voice. She would have liked nothing better than to take him home every day after work, and sit him in a chair to read for her all evening. She had long wondered in secret what it would be like to have that deep, warm voice read erotic literature to her by candlelight, accompanied by a large glass of red wine.

Mercedes Riemenschneider laid an encouraging hand on his. She wanted to hear this novel too, and not just on the off chance it might contain erotic passages involving a hot-blooded half-Cuban woman.

"But it's not for…"

"Read. Please. For me."

The Reader stared pleadingly at her. He would much rather have read the phone book, or the labels on the cigar boxes, even the ones translated into Serbian. She ignored his plea and walked back to her office, swinging her hips a little more than usual.

Tenderly, the Reader brushed the title page, as though the manuscript first needed to be gently woken.

"*Silent Tango,*" he began. "By..." He said something that sounded like two words, but although he had been a master of final syllable modulation since his speech training, no one understood his murmur.

His voice was suddenly as thin as fine yarn. He read the first few hesitant sentences as if testing each word for its stability.

Carl and Schascha held their breath: they were the ones who had put this genial man in a less than genial situation.

But with each word that set out into the world without a stumble, with each sentence spoken aloud to an audience that did not yawn, or laugh in the wrong place, the Reader's confidence grew, and from that confidence was born a pleasure in the text, in his own words.

Carl and Schascha watched as the Reader glowed.

And they watched Mercedes Riemenschneider glowing in her office.

Even the employees had stopped what they were doing and were just listening. They could sense that something extraordinary was happening.

A world premiere at the Torcedor cigar factory.

And a man who had found his voice.

"I owe you a favor," said Carl. "Whatever you want. You've saved a writer's life today."

Carl and Schascha crept away, not wishing to disturb the Reader in his moment of triumph. Carl, too, felt elation coursing through him in quantities he had not realized his old body could still process. At Münsterplatz, he bade a warm farewell to Schascha, who ran quickly to school. To celebrate the occasion, Carl bought himself a Silvaner from the famous Würzburger Stein vineyard, and even had a sip at lunchtime. Then he read his favorite novel, *The Uncommon Reader.* A slim volume by a renowned author, he allowed himself to read it only once a year, looking forward to it each time like a connoisseur anticipating the first asparagus of the season.

So far, it had been one of the best days of Carl's life. But sometimes life doesn't allow us too much happiness all at once, as if it was a commodity to be frugal with, for fear of hubris.

That evening, at the City Gate bookshop, Sabine Gruber asked him into her office. He sat down; she remained standing.

"I have some wonderful news," said Carl, wanting to share the morning's events. She was sure to be pleased that her bookshop brought such happiness into people's lives.

She did not respond. "Before you hear it from anyone else, the funeral will be restricted to a very small circle of people. Close family only. It's what Father would have wanted. Please wait until the official funeral service is over to offer your condolences at the graveside. No wreaths."

"But surely the whole city will want to say goodbye to Gustav!" Carl could no longer stay on the chair. "The cemetery will be full—he loved all his customers." Well, perhaps not all, but most of them. No one loved everybody, not even a man with as much sense of humor as Gustav.

"It was his wish."

"I don't believe you!" The words burst out before Carl could stop them.

"Are you calling me a liar?"

"No." He shook his head. "I just think you may have misunderstood him."

"It didn't sound like it. That's an end to this conversation. I suggest you consider carefully what you accuse me of in future." Sabine Gruber left him alone. And Carl felt more alone, and more lonely, than ever before in this bookshop—his bookshop.

He was about to get lonelier still—in the bustle of Münsterplatz, where Schascha usually joined him. Carl waited a long time, finally combing the square for her, and even calling her name. In the end, he had to walk his route alone. He even walked past houses where he had no new book to deliver. Maybe Schascha was waiting for him at Mr. Darcy's? Or at Effi's? Or with the Reader? Carl even peered into the dark alleyway he feared so much. There was no sign of Schascha anywhere. Even Dog declined to appear that day. Twice now, he'd not given it a treat, so that was an end to its affections.

When Carl returned to Münsterplatz, there was still no Schascha to be seen.

Some people stop eating when they are unhappy. The following day, Carl stopped reading. He ate on autopilot, but reading didn't have an automatic mode. He tried several times, wanting to direct his thoughts into another world, but they clung fast to the here and now. Carl couldn't remember a day when he'd read nothing, ever since he'd first learned to decode the arrangement of letters into words. But reading was an activity with a mind of its own. It couldn't be forced.

That evening, as he arrived at the City Gate bookshop, he could see Sabine Gruber through the glass, talking to a wildly gesticulating man in work overalls. She was attempting to calm him, but without success—quite the opposite, in fact. He now appeared to be shouting, the large windowpanes vibrating at the sound. Emotional outbursts were a rare sight in bookshops. While you might find hundreds, maybe thousands, in the novels on the shelves, they were uncommon in the aisles.

As the man exited the bookshop, he tried to slam the door behind him, but it resisted, closing as softly as usual.

Shaking his head, Carl entered the shop. The bell had not stopped tinkling before Sabine Gruber asked him to step into her office. Once inside, she didn't look him in the eye, nor did she face him.

Carl didn't have the time to sit; there wasn't even enough

time to take a breath. The moment they were alone, Sabine Gruber uttered a single sentence: just two words, one syllable each, but with more impact than an entire novel.

"You're fired." Her voice was trembling with rage.

"What? Why?"

"I don't have to give a reason, nor do I wish to." She stood behind her desk as if it was a barricade.

"Effective wh-when?" Carl stammered. He had expected this, and feared it too, but not so soon. It felt unreal.

"Immediately. I will inform your customers by phone directly."

After all these years, he was to disappear without a word, like a book that ends midsentence. It couldn't be true.

"Please let me do that in person today!" When Sabine Gruber gave no response, he added, "I won't cause any trouble; I'll tell my colleagues I accept the decision. If you like, I'll tell them I resigned."

She gave no reply, but nodded and pointed to the door.

And that was the end of Carl Kollhoff the bookseller.

The knowledge that you're doing something for the last time lends even the simplest tasks an air of significance. Never before had Carl folded the corners of the packing paper into such sharp creases, or aligned the edges so precisely. He saved Effi's book for last, wrapping it with such care and tenderness, he might have been swaddling a baby. Holding it in his hands, he couldn't help thinking how light it was. A whole life story was contained within its pages, yet it weighed less than a pound.

As Carl slid it into his backpack, his throat constricted. What a stupid old man he was. He'd known his work here would one day end, yet still he'd hoped it would never happen. He also knew he'd die one day, but he couldn't imagine that either. Of course he'd had decades to get used to the idea, but he guessed some things needed a little more time. A few thousand years ought to do it.

Carl looked around the cluttered, windowless back room, stacked high with publishers' catalogs, remaindered books awaiting return, and trays of promotional materials for long-outdated new releases. The room had always been a warm, safe burrow to him.

He took the rear exit.

Again, he waited in vain for Schascha, but this time he didn't wait long. It was good she wasn't there to accompany him today; it would only have made everything more difficult. She wouldn't have allowed him to turn away his sadness like an uninvited guest. Carl wanted this final round with a backpack full of books to be an entirely normal, average walk, indistinguishable from all the others that had preceded it. A walk where melancholy didn't tag along, only the gentle, calm pace of the everyday. Carl walked neither more quickly nor more slowly than usual, nor did he hesitate when ringing a doorbell for the final time. Mr. Darcy was the first on this final round. Carl was glad, knowing the man would receive the farewell in a composed manner, like the English gentleman Carl saw in him.

He was unaware that tears had begun streaming from his eyes. Viewed under a microscope, emotional tears look different from those we produce as a reflex to strong winds or chopped onions, which prevent our eyes from drying out, or irritants from entering. Yet as far as we know, crying is unknown in the animal kingdom—it's uniquely human. Wherever we are from, whatever language we speak, all humans cry. From that perspective, Carl had not been human for many years, since the day he had forgotten how to cry.

That was the thought that shot through Carl's mind as Mr. Darcy opened the heavy door.

"Mr. Kollhoff, is everything all right? You're crying."

"Am I?" He wiped the tears from his eyes, and stared astonished at his damp fingertips. "I am."

"Did the wind blow something into your eye?" Mr. Darcy hoped Carl would answer in the affirmative. He lacked the experience for consolatory conversation.

"There must be something wrong with my tear ducts," said Carl, avoiding the question. He pulled Mr. Darcy's book from his backpack, handing it over with trembling hands.

"You've wrapped it with great precision today."

"I was in the mood for it."

"It's always a good day when I see you, and get a new book! Opening it is like meeting a new friend." He looked around. "Speaking of friends, is Schascha not with you today? Did I bore her so much last time with my floral clock, she doesn't want to come again?"

Carl didn't want to think about it. "How did you like *Pride and Prejudice*?"

"Quite wonderful! I read it three times in succession, I've been completely lost in it the past few days. Do you know why?"

"I suspect because it's so well written."

"That too, but chiefly because I recognized myself in one of the characters."

"Oh?"

"Yes. Charles Bingley. Of course, I'm older than him, but otherwise we're extremely alike. You knew that when you chose the book for me, didn't you?"

Carl gave a tired smile. "What we know, and what we believe we know, are sometimes two different things."

"Would you like to come in for a moment? We could talk

about the book." Mr. Darcy opened the door wide in invitation.

"Sadly, I have no time today; I have a lot of customers to get to. But another time, I'd love to." *If you would even want a former bookseller in your house*, thought Carl. "There's something else I must tell you." He took a deep breath. "In future…"

"Yes?"

His mouth was dry. His heart was dry. His whole world was dehydrated.

"Can I offer you a whisky?"

"In future…" Carl began again, closing his eyes to make the leap to the next words. "In future…"

His throat closed, his vocal cords stiffened, his whole body refused to cooperate. He couldn't force the truth out.

He gave up, and retreated into a lie.

"In future, I'm sure I'll have time for it. Who knows how much time we have left to us."

"Are you ill, Mr. Kollhoff?"

He stared at Darcy for a long moment. "Only the illness we call age. I must get on. Take care!"

Mr. Darcy laid a hand on his shoulder—something he'd never done before. "You too, Mr. Kollhoff. I mean that from the bottom of my heart." He couldn't tell what was weighing so heavily on Carl, but he could sense something was very wrong. But Darcy was a man who didn't like to be pressed to open up, so he allowed Carl his silence and simply handed him the next book order on a slip of paper.

Carl left, his head bowed like Atlas, carrying the weight of the heavens on his shoulders.

"I'm such a weak old fool," he said to Schascha, who wasn't there. "As if I could hide from the truth! Truth is a bloodhound that will find me out."

Around the next corner, Dog appeared, barking a greeting. Carl wondered whether life was trying to tell him something.

"Hello, you." He stroked the little head that stretched toward him. "I'm much more fond of you than I am the truth." Carl patted his empty pocket. "Sorry, no treats for you. Thought you weren't coming back."

Dog stayed with him all the same. It suddenly occurred to Carl that he didn't live in a city of thousands of inhabitants at all—he lived in a village, one that only he was aware of: the village of readers. At first glance, the houses in the village didn't stand directly next to one another. In reality, they were like the ribs of an accordion, at a distance from one another when the instrument was drawn apart. As soon as the music began to play, and the bellows pressed the air out, they suddenly found themselves next to one another. On his walks, the spaces between the houses, and the people living in them, disappeared. It made no difference whether he took two paces from one to the next, or a hundred. These houses belonged together. The inhabitants of this village of readers themselves knew nothing of their connection. Only Carl.

At each of Carl's customers, the same scene played out as at Darcy's. At Effi's, where her doorbell was working again, and her face flawless, but her eyes as overcast as a sky full of rain clouds. At Mrs. Longstocking's ("sourdough beard"); at Doctor Faustus's, who had hung Schascha's puppy calendar on the wall, but continued to hold dogs' lupine heritage against them; at Hercules's, where he sat at the kitchen table explaining the letters *a* to *d* to Carl with such enthusiasm, you'd think humanity had only just invented these extraordinary symbols; at Sister Amaryllis's, who told him serial killers were her favorite, especially if they were Catholic and murdered in line with biblical doctrine. And at the Reader's, who had a thank-you gift for Carl in the form of a copy of *Silent Tango*, bound with sewing thread. His boss had been so thrilled, she had invited him to her house the following Saturday to read the magnificent first chapter all over again—complete with its dance scene sizzling with erotic tension.

For each of them, it was simply another day on which Carl Kollhoff the bookseller walked to their door.

For Carl, it was the first day he spent as an echo of his former life.

As he shut his door, fear grasped hold of him like a giant hand, shaking his whole body from head to toe, hurling every last spark of happiness out of him.

chapter 6

Tracks

CARL BOUGHT THE BOOKS.
He received no money on delivery; his customers had long since moved to bank transfer direct to the bookshop's account. It would only come to light at the year end when the lovely tax adviser from Lovenberg, Müller & Czöppan pointed it out.

To enable him to buy enough books, Carl sold his own. Every day, more disappeared from his shelves; all the paper-and-ink friends that had shared his home for years—decades—were gradually moved out of his apartment. Carl didn't have the heart to hand them over in person to Hans at the antiquarian bookshop, so he paid Leon, the work experience lad, to do it, waiting for him outside the City Gate bookshop at closing time. He received almost nothing for his treasures. Sometimes a new book cost him twenty old ones, and his customers were ordering more than ever before. It was their way of easing his distress.

Carl attended Gustav's funeral from a distance. It was a

small group of mourners: just three people to accompany the old bookseller on his final journey. Carl waited until they had disappeared, then stood by the graveside to give his old friend a few volumes of *Winnetou* and *Old Shatterhand*: valiant heroes who would watch well over him. *Paper is carbon,* he thought. *We humans are the same. Books and humans are made of the same stuff.*

He continued gifting his customers books too, which only served to empty his shelves even faster. Darcy received Jane Austen's complete works. After giving Effi a number of books about women who left their husbands, Carl began giving her crime novels about women who murdered their husbands instead. Poison seemed to be the preferred method. Not that Carl wished to encourage her to commit such an act; he merely wanted to show where it could all lead if she didn't leave.

"You must stop giving me these books—everything is wonderful here," said Effi. Her husband had told her the exact words she should choose. He had found the novels, and read the back covers. He'd immediately thrown the books away, along with Effi's favorite novels. "I'm afraid you've gained completely the wrong impression," she continued.

Carl could see there were no longer any flowers behind her in the hallway. Not a single cut flower or houseplant—not a living thing to be seen.

Effi closed the door quickly. It had been too many lies all at once, and they weren't as attractively packaged as the books.

As he stood alone at the closed door, Carl missed Schascha's cheery chatter. It had always put him in mind of the rattling of a water mill as a small stream runs through it, glinting in the sunlight. So he talked to her, and she talked back.

"That was a lie," said Schascha. "You didn't get the wrong impression at all."

"I know, but she's not lying to us, she's lying to herself."

As they continued their route, Schascha drove him on when his footsteps dragged. She said, "You need to walk faster, or the books will go bad." As they approached Pino's, she told him in a strict voice, "No ice cream today, you need the money for books. They're a foodstuff with a longer shelf life."

Carl realized this couldn't go on: he needed the real Schascha.

He couldn't phone or visit; she'd never told him her surname, or pointed out the building in which she lived.

He decided the following day he would visit all the school playgrounds in the city, eyes peeled, and ask children in Schascha's age group if they knew a little girl with dark curls. Schascha, once met, was never forgotten.

Carl had climbed Mount Everest and dived into the Mariana Trench. He had traveled remote regions of Kurdistan and conducted research in the icy Antarctic. His books had given him all these experiences. Mercifully, they had spared him the world of German elementary schools.

Such a chaotic maelstrom of small, running human beings! As a child, Carl had once found an ant heap in the forest, and had returned again and again for weeks to observe them. That had also been a great scurrying swarm, but it had had its own internal order. At the St. Leonhard School, on the other hand, the playground seemed to have produced a successful demonstration of chaos theory in action.

On his way to the entrance, Carl bumped into one child after another—or rather, they practically ran him over. Even worse than the turmoil was the shouting and yelling. Reading, in contrast, was a silent occupation. Even when the pages told tales of the war elephants used by Hannibal to cross the Alps in 218 BCE, there was no trumpeting to rattle the living room windows, or when the tanks of Rommel's Seventh Panzer Division broke through the Maginot Line near Maubeuge, his own breathing had still been the loudest sound in the room. He heard everything with his eyes.

When Carl finally made it into the building, he leaned against a wall and took several deep breaths. Then he asked his way to the school office, where he was informed they were not permitted to give out any information. Carl decided to ask the children.

The bell was just ringing for the end of recess, and a storm tide of students washed past him. One boy, roughly Schascha's age, was trotting slowly enough for Carl to speak to.

"Do you know a girl called Schascha?"

"What kind of a weird name is that?" asked the boy.

"I thought that's what children are called these days. Like they used to be Edeltraud or Gertrud."

"Nah, there's no one called that in this school. I have to get to geography." He'd forgotten his homework again, but he wasn't going to tell the crazy old man that.

Judging by Schascha's age, Carl knew she must either be in her final year of elementary school, or first year of middle school. Starting from Münsterplatz, he had marked all the potential schools on a city map. There were seven altogether. The St. Leonhard School had been number one.

Carl wasn't sure his ears and nerves would withstand all seven.

At the next one, he spared himself the walk to the office, deciding instead to speak directly to the students standing in the playground during recess. He asked both older and younger students, gave them Schascha's name, and described her as best he could.

He managed six. At the last, the Pestalozzi Middle School, he had spoken to three girls when the playground supervisor, in the form of a teacher in a Gore-Tex jacket zipped up to his chin, loomed in front of him.

"May I ask what, or who, you're looking for?"

"Schascha," replied Carl. "She's nine years old, and she has dark—"

"There's no Schascha here," the teacher interrupted him. "Please leave the school premises immediately, and don't ever try talking to our students again, or I'll call the police."

"But—"

"Who is this Schascha? Clearly not your granddaughter, she'd have told you where she goes to school."

"She's…" Carl faltered.

The playground supervisor took hold of his arm. "Are you confused? Should I phone someone for you?"

"Yes. No," replied Carl, sounding more confused than ever. "It's best I just go."

"I think you're right." He patted Carl on the back, like a knacker patting a horse's flank as it goes for slaughter.

The seventh school had closed, so he decided to visit his customers in search of Schascha. And because Carl could no longer bear her absence, he imagined her alongside him. She wore her yellow winter jacket, gleaming like new. Her little backpack was stuffed full, but she still hopped and leaped as if the road surface was made of rubber. She even talked all the while in his head. His replies, on the other hand, were not so confined.

First, he went to Mr. Darcy; that was, after all, where his round always began.

"I like Darcy a lot, especially his garden," declared Schascha.

"Then why didn't you say anything when he showed us his floral clock?"

"Silly old man," she said tenderly. "I was so excited because

I had a book to give him. I think I might be in his garden, in that awesome chair."

At Mrs. Longstocking's, Schascha said, "I'm here, for sure!"

"With a teacher?"

"She's not at school anymore. Teachers are only really horrible in schools, where kids can't escape them."

"That sounds terrible."

"It is. You've just forgotten, because it was so long ago. But Mrs. Longstocking is nice now. She's like a dragon that can't breathe fire anymore. I might be at hers, doing my homework."

"With no risk of being burnt to a crisp?"

"Now you've got it!"

When they reached Hercules's door, there was no more doubt in Schascha's voice. "Where else would anyone rather be than with a chap that powerful, who always offers you a drink too?"

"Since when did you say *chap* and not *guy*?" (Sometimes it came to Carl's attention that he was talking to himself, but he was always quick to find his way back into the narrative.)

"Guy, chap, it's all the same. I've decided to start using your old words, so you understand me."

"Thank you, that's exceptionally thoughtful of you."

She was at Doctor Faustus's home, because she wanted to take another look at the puppy calendar, particularly the September dachshund, and at the Reader's apartment to ask him to read her current book assignment out loud. When they arrived at Sister Amaryllis's convent, Schascha was positive she was behind the convent walls, as she had always wanted to be a nun—an assertion Carl found odd, but not inconceivable.

At every door, Carl asked, "Have you seen Schascha? Has she been here?"

No one had seen her. She had not visited anyone.

Everyone was concerned. Carl was not the only one to have developed a soft spot for the child.

He had saved Effi for last. Or perhaps Schascha had—Carl couldn't say for certain. It felt like approaching the final chapter of a book, and fearing it would not contain the anticipated ending.

"Why would I be at Effi's?" asked Schascha. "She's so unhappy, and her husband scares me."

"You're courageous, and you have a good heart. You want to help her."

"You have a good heart too, why don't you help her?"

"Because I'm too frightened," replied Carl, pulling his cloth hat low on his forehead. "That's why I've been living the same day over and over for decades. Only the minor details change. That's what anxious people do."

"I'm not a minor detail!"

"No, you're decidedly not," said Carl. "Now ring the bell."

She prodded a small finger into his chest. "D'you not even dare do that?"

"Just ring it."

It took Effi a while to come to the door. (This time, she hadn't been standing behind the door, but had come up from the basement.) She didn't look as perfect as usual: her eyes had dark circles and her skin was flushed.

"Mr. Kollhoff? Has something happened? You don't usually call at this time of day."

"Have you seen Schascha?"

"Is she missing?"

"Yes—well, I miss her..." The significance of the question hit him. Was she not just missing from his own world, but the wider world too? Had she disappeared? Had something happened to her? "Have you by any chance read anything in the paper, or heard anything on the radio?"

Effi shook her head. "Is she not at home?"

The fear began to expand in Carl's stomach like air in a leather ball. "She always meets me in Münsterplatz."

"I'm sure she's fine. Maybe she's on a school trip."

"She would definitely have told me. Schascha's not the kind of girl to simply not come. She's so reliable!"

Effi stroked Carl's hand gently. "Mr. Kollhoff, I would love to help you look for her, but my hands are…" She could say nothing further. "I'm so sorry." She closed the door without another word.

In fact, from that moment on, there wasn't another word from anyone. Schascha had fallen silent too.

Carl delivered no books that evening.

Neglecting his round had the same effect on Carl's life as removing a small pebble that secures a whole wall. He struggled to get to sleep, then slept through the rattling of his old alarm clock the following morning. When he did wake up, he gazed in horror at the clock face, before dressing hurriedly and setting out, without shaving or eating breakfast, to the last of the seven schools—Schascha had to be there. His visits to educational establishments on the previous day had caused him such stress, he attempted to calm himself with the thought that he would be surrounded by books—tucked into schoolbags or lying on tables—even if they were only schoolbooks, which weren't designed for calming anybody.

At the Carl Orff School, as the bell rang for recess and children streamed out into the yard, he stood by the double doors, calling Schascha's name over and over. Each yellow coat made him jump and shout louder; each shock of dark curls that came bobbing around the corner made him crane his neck.

Soon the stream of children became a trickle, and Carl began to question individual students. At least, that was what he imagined he was doing; in reality, it bore more resemblance to an interrogation. "Schascha must be here; tell me where I can find her!" Or, "Is Schascha still inside? Is she ill? You must know!"

None of the children knew anything about Schascha, but they did know a lot about how to run away from Carl. This time it was the caretaker who drove him away, wielding a broom with all the menace of an experienced martial arts practitioner.

Carl went to the nearest discount store.

He paused at the Franconian Bocksbeutel, then picked a box of cheap Italian table wine from the lowest shelf. His fingers weren't in the mood for gliding over the elegant curves of a bottle; they settled for the sharp edges and corners of a carton. He had barely stepped back out onto the pavement before he tore the carton open and began to drink.

On his way home, he passed the railings outside the St. Leonhard School. The laughter and cheerful squealing of children drifted across, mocking him. He looked away. Something yellow flashed in the corner of his eye. He ignored it.

Then a child shouted, "Give me back my book!" and he turned, as if a book in peril was his concern.

And there she stood.

Not wearing her yellow winter coat. Nor had it been Schascha's voice that he heard; that had been a red-haired boy standing nearby, desperately trying to reach a schoolbook that a taller boy was holding above his head, snatching it away each time he jumped.

Carl could read Schascha's lips, as they formed the words "It's the Book Walker!"

She ran to the railing. "You've been looking for me, haven't you?"

Joy bubbled up in Carl as fiercely as a shaken champagne

bottle that had just been uncorked. He was so happy, his heart ached. "I was worried. But now I've found you."

Schascha hugged him through the bars. "I've missed you so much, d'you know that?"

"I've missed you too."

"I've missed you more. To the moon and back!"

"That's from a book."

"Still true!" She beamed.

"I asked after you here yesterday, but nobody knew you."

"Did you ask for Schascha?"

"Yes, of course."

She grinned. "There's no Schascha here."

"But…?"

She pointed to her own chest. "Charlotte. I'm only Schascha to you. I've always wanted my friends to call me that, but they never did. I made the name up for myself." This was true, but not the whole truth. Charlotte had invented a superheroine for herself, because the boys in Class B were forever showing off at break time, pretending to be Captain America or Iron Man. She had imagined a woman flying over the town in a fluttering red cape, with yellow laser beams shooting from her eyes.

That was Schascha.

She looked exactly like her mother in the black-framed photo on the hall table. Charlotte always picked daisies on the way home from school to lay in front of it.

"I'm very pleased to meet you, Charlotte," said Carl, bowing. "It's an honor to be allowed to call you Schascha."

"I think so too!"

Carl threw the wine box in a garbage can. "Why did you stop coming?"

"Couldn't," said Schascha. Again, this was technically the truth, but was missing an important detail. Mrs. Disselbeck, the head teacher, had phoned home after Schascha had skipped two hours of school to go to the cigar factory. Schascha had confessed everything to her father, and he had forbidden her to ever go delivering books with Carl again. No amount of crying and begging had helped, nor all the notes she had written, covered in showers of hearts and pleaseprettypleases, nor the breakfasts in bed with toast cut into tree shapes with her Christmas biscuit cutters. Not even the packet soup dinners she had garnished so lovingly had any effect.

Although Schascha liked to talk as though words were popping candy fizzing on her tongue, she kept to herself the reason she hadn't turned up these past few evenings. And since a moment of silence would have given Carl the opportunity to ask, she filled the silence with something else instead.

"That's my friend Jule over there. She's my best friend forever—for now, anyway. She knows you too, and she says you have a funny neck, just like her grandpa."

Carl slid a hand over it. "I call it my turkey neck. You have to grow very old to get one of these; you're not ready to make the most of it at a young age."

"Make the most of it? How?"

"You need a turkey neck to do this." Carl flapped his arms as if they were wings, and gobbled like a turkey. The joy of having Schascha back was more intoxicating than any wine box.

Schascha barked with laughter, then looked around nervously to check whether any of her classmates had witnessed the spectacle.

The red-haired boy pointed at her and burst out laughing.

"That's Simon, isn't it?" asked Carl. "The one who's forever pushing you?"

Schascha nodded hesitantly. "Please don't go over!"

"Of course not; I'll deal with it in my own way."

"With books?" asked Schascha.

"Exactly. Do you know his address? Now I've seen him, I know exactly the right book for him."

Schascha scribbled it on the back of his hand. "But nothing embarrassing, okay? *Please!*" The bell rang. "I have to get back to class."

"Will you come join me on my round again?"

Schascha pressed her lips together. "Course."

"This evening?"

She nodded slowly, but said nothing more. Then she ran across the schoolyard, past the entrance door with its peeling red paint, and was gone.

On his way home, Carl passed by a small business selling tissue-paper flowers, and walked in on the spur of the moment. He asked for the kind that grow on treasure islands, or in the Wild West, or on the banks of the Mississippi, where Huckleberry Finn lived, but the saleswoman had no idea whether roses, tulips, field poppies, or carnations grew in those regions, and those were the only kind of flower they stocked. Carl took one of each, in an assortment of colors—Gustav had been a colorful character. The saleswoman wrapped the flowers carefully in paper when Carl told her they were for the cemetery. She shook her head, saying sadly they weren't designed for that; in the open air, they would lose their petals faster than real flowers.

"That's fine," replied Carl. "I only want to make an old friend laugh." Gustav had seen paper in many shapes, and printed with many words, but Carl was certain he'd never seen it folded into a floral display.

As he was closing the cemetery gate, he noticed Sabine Gruber standing at her father's grave. He turned right to sit on the cast-iron bench, where Schascha had shown him her friendship album, with its big thoughts about which book would make which person happy. The bench was quite close to Gustav's grave, but separated from it by a thick evergreen hedge—completely impenetrable to the eye, unless you found the right angle and knew in exactly which direction to look.

Sabine Gruber was kneeling by the graveside, which was marked by a temporary plain wooden cross.

"Look," she was saying, "here's what it will look like. The whole gravestone will be in the shape of an open book, and they'll engrave some lines about your life." Nervously, she tucked a strand of hair behind her ear. "I'm showing you something beautiful, but all I can imagine is you reproaching me about the funeral." Sabine Gruber screwed the sketch into a ball and stuffed it into her jacket pocket. "But I honestly thought it was the right thing to do! It wasn't until there were so few of us at your graveside that I missed everyone—and thought it must be sad for you. You always loved being surrounded by people. I'm sorry, all right?"

She pinched out a weed that had broken through the soil. "Sometimes I can't bear myself. And I'm sure I'm not alone. But I'm only trying to do things right. To make you proud of me. But now you won't ever be, no matter how hard I try. I had my chances, and you had yours. And we both wasted them, didn't we? When it comes down to it, I think fundamentally I lack your book gene. I could work till I sweat blood, and I'll still never be like you or your precious Carl. I can see it in his eyes, that I'm still just a little girl to him. Did you know he once complained to my German teacher because I got a D, and he thought I should have got an A? My friends found out. It was unbelievably embarrassing. He behaved as if he was my father. *You* were my father. Or maybe you weren't. He probably meant well—in fact, I'm sure he did, but I never asked him to do it. I don't need him, I can manage on my own. And stop giving me that grim smile. Can't you show me a little warmth, even now you're dead? A little understanding? No, you never were any good at that."

She looked up from the grave into the inky blue sky with a deep sigh. "Do you remember the time you got so upset that I'd drawn on the blank end pages of your books? They were all illustrations to match the titles. I'd made a really good job of Günter Grass's *Cat and Mouse*, but you were livid that I'd defaced your precious novels. I was a little child, for God's sake! But I never could compete with your books." She stood up. "Why did you have to be dead for me to tell you all this?" She zipped her jacket up noisily. "You know what the saddest part is? I love books, I really do. But they've never made me as happy as they did you. I couldn't ever forgive you for that." She hesitated, then brushed her hand over the wooden cross and walked away.

Carl waited until Sabine Gruber had left the cemetery before laying the paper flowers on his old friend's grave. Gustav would need time to process what had just been said. He'd always been concerned that his daughter didn't have what it took to run a bookshop. That was the reason he never let her get away with anything, hoping she would understand when she was older. Now that Gustav had discovered what an error of judgment that had been, there was no time left to put it right. There would be no sequel to their story together.

That afternoon, Carl emptied more bookshelves. Soon he'd be living all alone. At first, he'd gazed individually at each book, sensing its place in his heart; now they all disappeared without a glance into brown removal boxes. The proceeds would suffice for one more round.

Carl appeared in Münsterplatz that evening ahead of schedule, keeping a lookout for Schascha. She arrived slightly out of breath, but in a sunny mood. Her father was at a meeting with a colleague. Before he left, he'd cooked her a proper hot dinner with dumplings, peas, baby carrots, and a generous portion of gravy; he'd even had a gift for Schascha, as a reward for keeping to his ban on her meeting with Carl. It was a chessboard: he was keen to teach her to play. Schascha had been less than pleased, as she'd told him in no uncertain terms the previous year that yes, there was a chess club at school, but no, she wouldn't join it. She thought it was totally stupid.

Schascha fervently hoped the gift for Carl, which she now pulled out of her backpack, would be better received. "Here, this is for you." It was a rolled-up A4 sheet of paper tied with a red ribbon.

"Should I open it straight away?"

"Course! I want to see your face!"

Carl carefully loosened the ribbon and unrolled the paper. Before he even had time to inspect it closely, Schascha began to explain the colored-pencil picture.

"This here in the middle is you as a bookworm, that's Dog next to you, and you've got all your friends around you. Can you tell who they all are?"

"That's Darcy," said Carl, pointing to a worm standing in front of an imposing house. "Effi" (worm with flowers); "Hercules" (worm with dumbbells); "Reader" (worm with cigar); "Doctor Faustus" (enormous glasses); "Sister Amaryllis" (nun's habit); "Mrs. Longstocking" (standing behind Hercules, pointer in hand). "That's very kind of you."

"Do you like it?"

"I love it! May I give you a hug?"

"Course! You don't need to ask. I usually just do it."

It felt good to hold her like this, even if Carl didn't really know where to put his arms. On the other hand, Schascha had a much better idea of what to do—she was a hug expert. And just like dancing, it was important that one person could do it right, because then they could lead.

"You know," said Carl, "bookworms are very rare creatures, and usually extremely timid. An endangered species in urgent need of protection."

"I'll protect you!"

"Can I ask you a favor?"

"Course!"

"Could you add my most important worm to the picture?"

Schascha loosened her grip and took the sheet of paper. "Who did I forget?"

Carl laughed. "Yourself!"

She shrugged. "Oh, I'm not important."

"You're the most important of all," said Carl.

"Race you to Mr. Darcy's!" Schascha darted off, then stopped and turned, laughing. "Only kidding! You wouldn't stand a chance against me anyway."

Carl ran.

Schascha was right: he had no chance—and no breath left by the time he arrived at the villa. Schascha gave him no time to get his breath back; she was already ringing the bell.

Mr. Darcy answered the door almost immediately with a beaming smile. "'The person, be it gentleman or lady, who has not pleasure in a good novel, must be intolerably stupid.'" When Carl gave him a quizzical look, he added with a smile: "My favorite quote of the day! It comes from Mr. Tilney in *Northanger Abbey*." He waved them in. "I have something to show you. Particularly you, Schascha. Most especially you!" He walked quickly down the long hallway to the large living room with its window to the gardens, stretching away to the floral clock.

Carl and Schascha noticed it immediately: Mr. Darcy no longer lived alone. He had installed a wooden bookshelf, on which stood all of Jane Austen's novels. Now he had the constant company of Fanny Price, Anne Elliot, Catherine

Morland, Elinor and Marianne Dashwood, as well as Emma Woodhouse and, of course, Elizabeth Bennet. He may not have been able to watch them while they read, but at least he could read about them.

But just as a fire burning in a grate makes you notice how cold it is at your back, now that Mr. Darcy had all these books, and all the life they contained, he sensed how little of that life prevailed around him in the villa's rooms. Having the novels for company caused him joy and sorrow in equal measure.

"Please, sit down." He paused. He had used the formal *Sie*, as usual. "I think it's high time we used less formal modes of address. We've known each other for long enough, haven't we, Mr. Kollhoff? I may be the younger of the two of us, but I don't wish to let any pride of place stand in the way of our happiness. I've learned this from our dear Jane!"

He held out his hand. "Christian."

Fitzwilliam, thought the Book Walker mildly, before responding, "Carl."

"Please, sit down." This time, his words were less formal. For his standards, Mr. Darcy was in positively high spirits. "I had an idea last night. Why don't we start a book club? You know, where everyone reads a book together and talks about it. The same as in the past, when people sat together around the fire to tell one another stories. In the Stone Age, it might have been the warmth that gathered them together, but it was the stories that first gave them civilization. What do you think? Should we put up a poster? There's enough room here. In the summer, we could sit in my grounds. After the rain, at least."

Schascha was enormously proud that Mr. Darcy included her in this "we." It made her feel a whole ten years older. On the other hand, she felt a whole ten years wearier at the prospect of talking about books with other people—she had more than enough of that in her classes at school.

Carl was not fond of groups of people: they made him uncomfortable. Besides, he was the Book Walker, not the Book Talker. But how much longer could that continue? In that moment, he could no longer avoid reality: only a very few more book rounds lay ahead of him. And without books, he would cease to walk. He delivered books: that was his life. Without books, that life would be no more.

Unable to bear the thought any longer, he stood to go.

"I'm afraid we must get going," he said.

"And what do you think Mr.—" He corrected himself. "Carl. What do you think of my idea?"

"I think you should do it Mr.— Christian."

"You should so do it!" Schascha chimed in. She had no trouble using an informal *du*. "I'll spread the word, then you won't need a poster."

Carl walked quickly to the door.

"Next time, please bring me Jane's unfinished novels—*The Watsons*, *Lady Susan*, and *Sanditon*. I can't get enough of her at the moment." Mr. Darcy was eager to start the book club off straight away with these fragments.

"We will!" said Schascha—Carl was already out of earshot. She didn't catch up with him until he got to the corner. "Why did you run away?"

"We have a lot more books to deliver today."

"You're weird. Weirder than usual."

"Walking helps," said Carl. "Then the weirdness leaks out through the feet."

Schascha laughed, but only to release the tension in the air. Just like crying, she could also laugh on demand—although strangely, crying felt better.

With every step, Carl rapped the tip of his umbrella hard on the cobblestones. He was powerless to alter his miserable situation, and furious at the thought. There was no way to avert the end of his time as Book Walker.

As Dog joined them, Schascha was ready to leap in the air for joy. She quickly gave it a tiny, mouse-shaped treat she had bought precisely should this opportunity arise. The assistant at the pet shop had told her cats went wild for it. Schascha hoped Dog would make an exception, and be a cat, just this once.

"Are we going to see Doctor Faustus today?"

"He hasn't ordered anything. Why?"

"We have to go there. Right away!"

"But our route goes—"

"I know, but we have to go. Pleaseprettyplease!"

"You're making that face again—the one I can't refuse."

"Exactly. So do you give in?"

Carl gave in, and not long after, they were ringing Doctor Faustus's doorbell. When he opened up, the doctor rubbed his eyes in bewilderment, as if this would make the two figures at his door disappear. He searched his mind, wondering whether he had, after all, ordered that obscure historical treatise on Moses, with biblical delivery times. But no, a volume that consisted *exclusively* of mistakes was an insult to his intellect.

"How agreeable to see you," he said: Doctor Faustus was fond of using archaic expressions. "What brings you here?"

Carl looked expectantly at Schascha.

"We need your help," she said. "It's about this cat. It needs somewhere to stay for a week."

"Why?"

Um, oh yeah, why? pondered Schascha, who had imagined Doctor Faustus immediately agreeing and scooping Dog up in his arms. In her mind's eye, he'd even nuzzled his face into Dog's side, whereupon Dog had barked loudly with sheer pleasure.

In a moment of inspiration, she remembered what had happened that day with Simon at school.

"He, I mean, the cat, is being chased and picked on by other cats. And he, I mean she, I mean it, is totally innocent! They call it harassment!" She handed him the treats. "Here, these are Dog's favorites."

"Dog?"

"Cat! I'll bring you my old cat litter tray tomorrow. Till then, newspaper will do." At least, that's what the woman in the pet shop had said.

"Why are you bringing it to me? I have no expertise with pets."

"You're the only one of Carl's customers who lives far enough away from the other cats' territory. Dog—I mean Cat—will only be safe with you."

"Hmm."

Some people would have been daunted by a "hmm." In Schascha's world, it meant she'd won.

"Just one night, on trial? Or two?"

"Very well."

"Awesome, thank you! And don't be surprised if Do—if Cat makes some strange noises. It's supposed to." She tugged at Carl's sleeve. "We can't stop! Bye!"

Carl almost stumbled as he let her pull him along. He felt like a child who'd just broken into a chewing gum vending machine. "You think it will work?"

Schascha shrugged her shoulders. "Maybe! And if not, at least I've tried to make him happier. If Dog can't help him get over his dislike of dogs, no one can."

"But it's a cat."

"Exactly."

They were standing in front of Effi's house.

From which screams were emerging.

So loudly, the pigeons on the roof were flapping and fleeing in panic.

Carl took off his backpack and took out Effi's book. Then he walked resolutely to the door. But each time he tried to ring the bell, a new scream rang out, making him flinch away. They were sharp, clear screams—the kind that are uttered in reaction to pain. And they were screams that held no hope of an end to the pain.

Eventually, Carl's head drooped.

"Sometimes," he said, giving Schascha a troubled look, "a book is not enough. Not all wounds can be bound with paper. We need to find a public telephone."

"No, we don't." She unlocked her phone and handed it to him. "Touch the green phone icon." When he still hesitated, she tapped it for him.

Carl called the emergency number, asked for the police, and gave the address. After multiple prompts and a certain amount of hesitation, he also gave his name. Once he had been assured that help would be sent immediately, he handed the phone back to Schascha. "I don't know how to hang up if I can't put it back on the hook."

"What hook?" She ended the call.

Carl looked around. Where was there a good view of Effi's house, without being seen? He spotted a large container in front of a nail studio that was having a clear-out. Schascha had to stand on tiptoe and pull herself up a few centimeters with her hands to see over the cold metal sides.

It was ten minutes before a patrol car pulled up in front of Effi's house. Schascha's toes were numb, and her fingers were ice-cold.

Two police officers got out and rang the bell. A curtain twitched, then the door opened to reveal Effi and her husband. He had both hands on her shoulders, close to her neck, exerting a faint pressure.

"We're sorry to disturb you, but we received a report of screams coming from your house." The officer looked at Effi. "A woman's screams. The caller suspected you were being beaten. Or is there another woman in the house?"

"It's all a misunderstanding," said Effi's husband with a laugh. "I had the TV turned up loud."

"Is that true?" the officer asked Effi.

"Yes," said Effi, smiling.

"I'd never hit you, would I, darling? Tell the officer."

"He wouldn't," said Effi, smiling.

The officer gave her a searching stare. "Would you like to speak to us alone?"

"No, she wouldn't. We have no secrets from one another. That's what a good marriage is all about. And that's what we have." He gave her a firm kiss on the cheek.

Effi winced: it was exactly the spot he'd just hit her.

"What's the matter with your cheek?" asked the officer.

"Toothache," said Effi, smiling.

Once again, the officer held her gaze for a long time.

"We really appreciate you coming out." Effi's husband crossed his arms. "It's good that you follow up calls like this. But in this case, it's a false alarm. So the next time someone calls because I've got the TV up too loud, you'll know to save yourselves the trouble of coming out." He poked Effi. "Isn't that right, darling?"

"Yes. I'm sure there are other women who really do need your help," said Effi with a smile.

"Is that it then?" asked her husband. "We'd like to get back to the film. The ending is supposed to be the best part. I'll turn it down, of course."

Carl stepped forward from behind the container. His body

resisted: it made his heart beat fast and his knees tremble. But Carl's will was stronger than his body. "They're both lying! He hits her. I heard it. That was no TV."

"Huh, the bookseller," said Effi's husband. "I might have known. No more ordering books from the psycho, darling, or my hand might slip for real." He laughed.

Effi laughed too. Her entire body ached with the effort.

The officers looked at Carl. They didn't see the sincere, conscientious man he was; they saw an old guy in shabby clothes, looking out at the world with an expression of mild confusion.

Which indeed was what Carl was doing, because right now, this was a world he no longer understood.

"Next time, please make sure you're not calling us out for a TV," said one of the officers to Carl. "Of course, we'd rather turn out one time too many than one time too few, but we can only do something if a victim of domestic violence will talk to us." He seemed to be talking to Effi, rather than Carl, but her husband had already closed the door firmly, and was now lowering the shutters on the windows facing the street.

Carl didn't say a single word all the way to Sister Amaryllis's convent, despite the fact that Schascha produced a continuous stream of suggestions on how to rescue Effi. They ranged from breaking and entering, to hiring a private detective (or a girl gang who took on detective assignments).

The nun took one look at him, downcast and with shoulders hunched, and asked whether someone had hurt him.

At that, Carl broke down. The hard shell enclosing his feelings shattered, and all his fears for Effi, and his sense of failure, came tumbling out. He didn't stop talking until Amaryllis gently laid a hand on his arm.

"All shall be well."

"No, it won't, not at all!"

Sister Amaryllis straightened her nun's habit. "I'll go to her."

"You can't! You'll never get back into the convent!"

"Ah, it will be fine. Do you see anyone watching me? I've been worrying all this time for no reason."

"But—"

"No buts! What kind of a nun would I be, if I stayed cowering in fear behind solid walls instead of standing by someone who needed help?"

"What will you do?" asked Schascha. "The police couldn't do nothing."

Sister Amaryllis disappeared into the depths of the convent, to return a short while later with a Bible. "The Word of God is the strongest weapon." She could see the doubt in Carl's and Schascha's eyes. "And if speaking it aloud is not enough, it's great for throwing." She winked at them, stepped onto the street, and closed the door behind her. Then Amaryllis caressed the stonework softly, as if it were a beloved pet she was leaving at home alone. She gave a short sigh, then looked at Carl. "Take me there!"

Schascha had already run ahead. "This way, it's not far. Come on!"

It was entirely clear to Schascha that everything would now be all right. Amaryllis was a nun, which made her almost a saint, like Saint Martin or Saint Nicholas, and saints were a kind of superhero. She didn't know exactly what superpowers a nun had—she certainly didn't shoot lasers from her eyes, and flying appeared to be out of the question, but she was definitely different from normal people. And since all the normal people had failed to help Effi, only an abnormal one was up to the task.

Sister Amaryllis didn't believe in pausing for breath. She walked straight up to the house that Schascha pointed out, and knocked on the door. There was a doorbell, but she decided that a loud determined knock would have more effect.

"Who's there?" shouted a harsh male voice.

"My name is Sister Maria Hildegard. I've come from St. Alban's Benedictine Priory."

"That doesn't even exist anymore!"

"I still exist, and therefore so does the convent."

"You're that mad nun." The voice was drawing closer. "We don't want to make a donation!"

"I'm not collecting money."

"We don't want to buy anything either."

"I have nothing to sell."

"We don't need anything!"

"Everyone needs God."

"Go away!"

"No, I shall stay. And I have all the time in the world. Your neighbors will see there's a nun standing on your doorstep and you're not letting her in."

The man let out a roar. "Has everyone gone crazy today? Andrea, you see to her. But make it quick. We're not finished, you and me. That thing with the bookseller won't be over for you for a long time."

Effi smoothed her clothes, making everything look as neat and tidy as it should. She smoothed her hair, then her face. She put on the expensive white high-heeled pumps that made her look like she was going to a dance. Finally, she put on the charming smile that she practiced every morning in front of the bathroom mirror until her cheeks hurt.

Only then did she open the door.

In front of her, she saw not a nun, but a woman who had been locked in for a long time. A woman who had locked herself in a prison of her own choosing.

A woman who had left that prison today.

From first sight, they knew everything about one another.

"Come," said Sister Amaryllis, holding out her hand. "Now. It's time."

And Effi went. Just like that. That was the beautiful thing about walking: it was so very simple. If she didn't think about all the things that might follow, all the anguish and injuries, then the act of walking itself was child's play. It was simply putting one foot in front of the other, until suddenly she had left not just a house, but a marriage.

As long as she kept on walking.

And Effi did just that.

With Sister Amaryllis holding her hand, it was easy. Carl and Schascha fell in step with them, and Effi began to walk faster, glancing anxiously over her shoulder. But the door remained closed. When they had finally turned the street corner, she took a deep breath, and noticed her racing pulse for the first time. Effi smiled, and the smile was genuine. She could feel she was using completely different muscles for it. Sister Amaryllis explained to her in calm tones that they would go into the convent, where she would be safe. That she could find peace there. She didn't need to believe in God; it was entirely sufficient that God believed in her.

Two corners farther on, the convent appeared ahead of them.

Red-and-white tape was stretched across the entrance, and a building works sign had been placed in front. A workman was installing a new lock.

"All done," he said, as they reached him. He gave Sister Amaryllis a nod of greeting. "Sorry, just doing my job."

"How did you know I wasn't there anymore?" The nun's voice was composed.

The workman pointed to a small camera attached to the building opposite. The archdiocese had paid him good money to drop everything and turn out the moment the sister left the convent. The workman had paid a student to monitor any movement at night, although the young man had only actually kept watch for the first and last hour, and spent the rest of the time asleep.

"What about my things?" asked Sister Amaryllis. "My clothes? And what about my plants? They need watering, or they'll wilt!"

"Ask the archdiocese. I'll be taking the new keys to them now. As far as I know, the refurbishment will start as soon as possible. It'll be converted into exclusive apartments. Like I said, I'm sorry, but there's nothing I can do."

"Yes, there is: you could let me back in."

He shook his head. "There's too much risk you'd stay in there. I have to go. Have a good..." He didn't bother to finish the sentence.

Carl, Schascha, Effi, and Sister Amaryllis looked at one another.

"Then we'll go to a hotel," said the nun decisively. "A convent is not a building; a convent is the people. We will be a convent in room 27, or whatever other number we may be given." She had to keep moving. Coming to a halt felt like a new prison. Effi felt the same.

"Maybe it's for the best," said Sister Amaryllis. "Your husband is bound to suspect you're at the Benedictine priory after my appearance at your door; he won't think to look for you in a hotel. What divine providence that I couldn't get back in!" If she said it often enough, perhaps she would believe it. She had a lot of practice at believing. It wasn't as easy as people thought. Belief took a lot of effort—every day, given that real life had a tendency to contradict belief.

As they walked, Sister Amaryllis and Effi swung their hands, their fingers intertwined, like children on the way to school. Effi, in particular, enjoyed the lightness of it: it stood in such stark contrast to what had happened earlier.

Mr. Darcy's villa appeared on their left. Of all his many windows, light shone from a single one, hemmed in by the darkness of the others.

"Wait," said Carl, "perhaps there's another way." He gave Schascha a questioning look, and she gave him a thumbs-up.

It was only a few paces to the door, but Carl used each one to compose the words that would take Mr. Darcy by the hand and lead him with every syllable to the decision to take these two women into his home. It was important to formulate them very precisely. Darcy was still very much a solitary man, and undoubtedly easily overwhelmed.

As the door opened, Carl removed his hat, as was appropriate for a supplicant. The sudden exposure to sunlight and fresh air made the skin on his head twitch in confusion.

"Mr. von Hohenesch," he began, "I'm so sorry to disturb you, but—"

"Here's your book club," Schascha interrupted. "They'll live with you from now on, because they have nowhere else to go. You've got enough rooms, and they're both super nice."

Mr. Darcy hesitated for a moment, then opened the door wide in invitation.

They all sat together a long time in the large living room. Mr. Darcy attempted to cook something for his guests, but even fried eggs with fried potatoes have huge potential to go horribly wrong. At least he now knew his smoke alarm was functioning faultlessly.

The villa had so many guest rooms that the two new arrivals struggled to choose; they finally decided on two adjoining rooms with a view of the grounds, which Sister Amaryllis declared offered the perfect conditions for the cultivation of potatoes and radishes.

Carl and Schascha parted ways at Münsterplatz with a long hug, and a promise to meet the following day.

The following evening, she didn't appear.

This time, Carl wasn't worried. He told himself she was a child, and children were capricious by nature. You had to let them do their own thing and show them some understanding. It was a shame she had chosen not to come today, as he had brought a book for her Simon, and was keen to deliver it together with her. But it could wait for another day.

In a break from his usual routine, he didn't go to Mr. Darcy first; he wanted to make that stop the high point of the day. As he approached the dark alley that was a shortcut, Carl mulled over how good it had been to tread completely new paths over the past few days. Perhaps life was telling him he should continue?

He should step into the alley that had always struck such fear in his heart.

All would be well.

Carl took a deep breath. Everything in his life would be well.

He had no idea how, since he had emptied his final shelf that day. Not a single book remained to live with him. But he had packed the final volumes into the removal box for the antiquarian bookshop with a light heart. He would find a way; he was certain. Effi hadn't believed in one, nor had Sister Amaryllis, Hercules even less so. But even when a situation seemed hopeless, everything could turn around in a moment. He held on to that hope.

The alley in front of him was narrow and dark. *An old path for an old man*, thought Carl, and had to smile. At the end of it, he would walk into light that felt all the brighter. It would have been nice to have Dog beside him, but the cat was probably reveling in the luxurious accommodation at Doctor Faustus's home. The academic undoubtedly still had no idea he had fostered one of the quadrupeds he so feared.

In a city he knew like the back of his hand, stepping into the one alley he had never passed through, walking on the only cobblestones he had never trod, was a peculiar feeling. It was like discovering a secret room in an old house.

Carl looked around like a tourist. Each windowsill, every drainpipe fascinated him; everything seemed beautiful to him, despite the wan light. Today, he had gifted himself this alley.

Steps approached him from behind. As Carl turned around, he saw a figure step out of the shadows.

Carl recognized him. It was the man who had been arguing with Sabine Gruber at the City Gate bookshop, the night he had been fired.

Now the man was standing right in front of him.

He gave Carl's shoulders a hefty push. "Leave my daughter alone, you hear me?"

Carl was confused. "Who do you mean? Effi?"

"Don't make out you're stupid! You know exactly who I mean. Charlotte is *my* daughter! She spends time with *me*!" He pushed him again, and Carl stumbled back a few steps.

"She's helping me."

"She shouldn't be helping you, she should be staying at home and doing her homework, not trailing through the city with a cracked old man like you, or going to a cigar factory. She's still a child, for God's sake! For the last time: leave my daughter alone! Is that clear?" He pushed Carl again, this time firmly in the chest.

Carl was familiar with violence, of course. He had observed the bloody deeds of Jack the Ripper in London's East End, had flown in a Bell UH-1 Iroquois over skirmishes in the

Mekong Delta, had fought at Helm's Deep against Saruman's orc armies, and side by side with Arminius against the troops of Publius Quinctilius Varus in the Battle of the Teutoburg Forest. He had even watched Fat Man, the atom bomb, explode over Nagasaki, and been present as the Trisolarans had almost succeeded in vanquishing the entire united fleet of the human race with a single unmanned probe.

To Carl, violence was something he read about, not something he experienced. He had never learned how to react to violence. Books were his answer to everything.

"I have just the novel for you. It's quite wonderful." Carl took off his backpack, untied it quickly, and delved inside. He would give Schascha's father the book he had intended for Simon. It was about a formidable, headstrong, adventurous girl. It would help her father understand what an incredible daughter he had, and how he shouldn't shut her away in an apartment. The book was wrapped in dinosaur-print gift paper.

"Why do you hang around outside my daughter's school? Did you think I wouldn't hear about it?" Another push, harder this time. Carl almost lost his balance.

Carl put the book in the man's coat pocket.

"Did you push me? DID YOU JUST PUSH ME? You bastard, don't you dare push me!"

He was breathing heavily; tiny blood vessels had burst in his eyes. Carl thought he could see a tear, but couldn't figure out why. He didn't understand that before him stood a desperate father, filled with the fear of losing his daughter, or that he had perhaps already done so. A man who was not just shouting at Carl, but at the whole damn world that had allowed this to happen. He reminded Carl of Schiller's robber chief Karl Moor, an honest captain who becomes a criminal and commits terrible atrocities.

Fear began to blossom in Carl.

"If I see you one more time with my daughter, I'll kill you! Have you got that?"

"But—" began Carl. He wanted to explain how much good Schascha had done, that she was smarter than a whole reference section, that she could draw bookworms, and dogs that are cats; wanted to tell of how she could improvise in cigar factories, and run into villas so fast no one could catch her.

But Carl didn't get the chance.

Schascha's father pushed him with both hands, with full force against his chest.

This was a completely new form of push. It turned the world upside down: the evening sky was no longer above him, the ground no longer beneath him. He felt the cobblestones crash into his back like cannonballs, the final one connecting with his head. What little light there was in the alley blinked out.

chapter 7

Journey to the End of the Night

SOMETIMES ON HIS ROUND, particularly in summer, when the heat made the cobbles shimmer and he could get thirsty just from breathing, Carl would suck on small pebbles. They had to be round, to nestle neatly into his tongue, and large enough to prevent him swallowing them by accident: the kind that were ideal for skimming across the surface of a lake—eight times, at least. Carl found them on gravel drives, and would rinse them thoroughly before use in the only drinking fountain in the city. The difference in their flavor amazed him each time—after all, they were only stones. Then again, mineral water brands all tasted different too.

The pebble in Carl's mouth right now tasted bitter. His palate felt decidedly dull. Moving his tongue to push it aside, Carl found nothing but empty space: the stone had vanished. Had he swallowed it? Maybe he'd stumbled?

But he wasn't walking, was he?

He could hear a beeping sound. Why was there a truck reversing? Should he get out of the way?

Carl opened his eyes. Two walls of the room were painted a pastel yellow, while the rest of the room was white—wipe-clean surfaces everywhere. Next to him, a device was beeping with reassuring regularity. The other bed in the room was empty, covered with a layer of what looked like plastic wrap, like a bread roll delivered by a catering service. Sadly, nothing about the room said "party."

As Carl attempted to prop himself up, he realized his right arm was encased in plaster, as was his left leg. His head throbbed, possibly with the effort of processing the information.

There appeared to be a door leading to a corridor, and another leading to a bathroom. A TV, unplugged and dark, hung in one corner. Carl lay contemplating all this for a while. Then he fumbled for the wheeled bedside unit, and managed to open the drawer, where he found a remote control and a Bible—the Luther translation.

He'd been trying to give someone a book…

Memory flooded back. Schascha's father would surely turn up soon to apologize. And Schascha would bring him a book—hopefully one that hadn't been translated by Luther.

The door to the corridor opened, and a nurse in green uniform entered. When she saw Carl's eyes were open, she smiled.

"Good to see you awake, Mr. Kollhoff. I'm Sister Tanja."

"How do you know my name?"

"It's on your ID card, in your wallet." She pointed to Carl's olive green jacket hanging on the wardrobe door. "Besides, I know you from the bookshop. You introduced me to *Harry Potter*." And it was thanks to her enthusiasm for the boy wizard that she'd met her first boyfriend, she continued to chatter. The boyfriend had sadly proved to be an idiot. Harry Potter, on the other hand, had stayed with her to this day.

"What happened?" asked Carl.

"You had a fall. You have a minor break in your arm, and sadly a more major one in your leg. Besides that, concussion had you spark out for a few hours. Don't be hard on yourself—at your age, it's easy to take a tumble."

"But I didn't..." Carl began, then broke off. If he told her what had really happened, Schascha's father could be arrested; he might even lose his job.

"How did I get here?"

"Now there's an odd tale." The nurse grinned. "Well, not the part where the ambulance brought you to us, but the part before that—how you were found."

"Why? How did it happen?"

"Head up!" She plumped his pillow. "A woman living in Wilhelm-Tell-Gasse thought she heard a dog barking like crazy, and came out onto the street to see what was going on. She found you lying there, but there was no dog with you."

"It was a cat," said Carl. Tears pricked his eyes again. It seemed that now he'd relearned the art of crying, he'd never be rid of it again.

"How did you know that?"

"It reminded me of a good friend," he replied. "One who likes me for more than the food."

The nurse shook her head, deciding to attribute his response to the concussion.

Carl sent silent thanks through the window to Dog, whose endearing schizophrenia had undoubtedly saved him.

His eyelids felt heavy; they drooped closed again.

When he woke for the second time, everything looked exactly the same, but the evening had become a morning. Carl could feel his legs waiting to get going. They may not exactly have been racehorses champing at the bit, but years of habit were urging them to get away on their round. Carl looked about for his old shoes: so perfectly broken-in, he could feel every unevenness in the road surface through their soles. Even with his eyes closed, he knew exactly where he was in the city.

They lay in the far corner of the room, wrapped in a plastic bag.

He'd just need a little help putting them on. Once they were on his feet, everything else would happen of its own accord.

Carl did his round in his head. Everyone asked where he'd been, and he responded that it was nothing to worry about, he'd just had a minor accident.

The door opened, startling him.

Another nurse, wearing the same green.

"Hello, Mr. Kollhoff, I'm Sister Ravenna."

He propped himself up. "Could you just help me with my shoes please, then I'll be out of your hair."

She laughed. "Tanja told me you had a funny sense of humor. I'm afraid we need to keep you here a while longer yet."

Carl tried to swing his plaster cast out of bed. The pain that shot through his leg felt as though he'd touched a live wire. He groaned.

"No moving, rest up and get well. Head up." She plumped his pillow.

"Then I need you to tell everyone in the bookshop what's happened, so they can tell anyone who asks after me."

"Sister Tanja already did that yesterday. She told them you were here, and that it's nothing serious, to make sure no one worries about you."

His customers were sure to have asked at the bookshop, and would soon come to visit him.

"Do you have a book here? Any kind of book?" The nurse pointed to the drawer, and was about to say something when

Carl interrupted her. "Something not so heavy, maybe? I'll have to lift it with my left hand."

"Sorry, no. We don't have a patient library here. If you like, I can get you a magazine from the newsstand."

"Any chance they have Stevenson's *Treasure Island*? Or Karl May?" What was good enough for Gustav, was good enough for him.

"I think they've only got *John Sinclair: Demon Hunter*—our senior consultant buys them all the time. And some Disney paperbacks for the kids."

"I'll take one," said Carl.

It occurred to him he had no money.

"On second thought, don't bother."

Schascha would be here soon. She'd have a book for him. Or a calendar with puppies. And if she brought him another bookworm picture, he'd surely be allowed to pin it to the wall.

But Schascha didn't come. Nor did anyone else.

Not that day, nor any of the days that followed.

Just nurses, care assistants, and doctors. His room became a stage where the same roles were played by a rolling cast of actors. The performances took place at regular times each day, with small variations in the script. They helped him to eat, dress, wash, and urinate. It was fast, efficient, and occasionally a little less than gentle.

They didn't come to see him, only to see to him.

No one wanted to visit him.

In the evenings, Carl could sometimes hear barking from the city center. He told himself it was Dog missing him.

Did no one wonder why he no longer came to their door? Were they all so indifferent to him? Those people whom he'd seen more often than anyone else in the past few years?

No one visited, right up to the day he was discharged.

Carl hoped they would all be waiting at the entrance for

him, although he knew they would not be. All the same, he pictured the scene in the bright colors Schascha loved to use, painting each detail in his mind, each of them smiling brightly.

Standing alone in front of the hospital, nothing was familiar. His world didn't extend this far.

He had no money for a taxi, and too much pride to ask anyone in the hospital for some. He asked a passerby for directions to the minster and set off.

Over three kilometers on crutches, with frequent pauses, pains in his underarms, three small stumbles, and a few grazes, and he was home.

Closing the door of his top-floor apartment behind him, all he could do was sink to the floor and fall asleep where he lay.

The clothesline ran along the walls like a mountaineer's safety rope. Carl had stretched it taut across shelves and cupboards, knotting it tightly to window handles and radiators.

Next, he had turned his attention to the bookshelves. He could no longer bear their emptiness, so he drew book spines on the inner surfaces of the bookcases with a felt-tip pen. He knew exactly where all his favorites had stood. In the rare places where he had forgotten a title, he wrote that of some important work he should have read long ago. Works by the Marquis de Sade and Giacomo Casanova appeared in his bedroom, but only to confront those masters of erotic literature with the miserable reality of his own bed frame.

The titles of all these remarkable books only made him more acutely aware of the treasures he had lost.

And without books, the acoustics in his apartment were completely wrong. It echoed like a crypt. He stopped speaking aloud.

He no longer went out of doors. He had a few jars of Spreewald gherkins, mandarins, halved pears (in light syrup), and mild sauerkraut. He ate very little; he was rarely hungry. Every day, he ate a little less: he had decided to accelerate his disappearance to the point where his body would come to the conclusion that it was no longer worth waking up in the morning.

Carl did not fear death, and never had. The village where he was born and raised had sat just outside the city gates, and had supplied violets to the cemeteries. Death had been a close companion from his earliest youth, even if it had bloomed in bright colors.

On the third day, Carl pulled all the blinds down: he could no longer bear the view of the city he had once thought of as his own. Now it was unfamiliar and fraught with peril—no longer the city he had walked through for decades, the soles of his shoes wearing down the cobblestones, where people were kindly disposed toward him.

It was now a city where people threw him to the ground and forgot him.

Carl almost welcomed the times his head, arm, and leg flared with pain—it was his only distraction from the heartache.

He soon ceased to count the days. He pulled his belt in tighter, until finally he was forced to use a can opener to punch new holes in it. He no longer knew whether it was day or night—he simply lay on his bed staring at the ceiling, or dozing a little, before returning to brooding.

A Book Walker with no books and no walk is a nonentity, he thought. It was only to be expected that no one was aware of him anymore. He'd already ceased to exist.

He'd often dreamed of dying while reading, with a book in his hand so riveting, the transition from life to death passed him by unnoticed.

An out-of-date phone book was the only thing he had been unable to convert into cash.

He didn't really read it, but it was comforting to brush the tips of his fingers across the paper and gently turn the pages over.

After confronting Carl in Wilhelm-Tell-Gasse, Schascha's father had thrown all his nine-year-old daughter's books from their window onto the concrete of their apartment building's inner courtyard. Schascha screamed and wrapped herself around his legs to hamper him, but one after another they flew out of the window, opening their pages and fluttering in the wind like white doves, before crashing to the ground, scattering their feathers far and wide.

Schascha's entire world blurred behind tears. She continued crying long after her father had left the room shouting, until finally she became aware he was watching the news.

Schascha stole out of the apartment, crept down the stairs, collected her treasures from the courtyard, and put all the pages back in order. Back in her room, she hid them all in boxes under her bed, setting up a barricade of soft toys to stand guard over them.

From that day on, she was grounded. Every evening, she opened the window wide to keep watch on Münsterplatz, in the hope that at least she could wave to the Book Walker, but Carl never came.

It wasn't like him at all.

Then she had a strange dream about Carl, which she would have preferred to forget, because it filled her with dread.

She rang the bookshop. They told her Carl didn't work for them any longer. Besides, they were very busy right now. No, they couldn't give her his address—they weren't an information service. Schascha could hear the irritation in Sabine Gruber's voice; she couldn't know that she was the latest in a long line of people asking after Carl. There seemed to be more every day; even people who had never bought a book, but for whom the man in green with the cloth hat who set off on his round every evening at seven was as much a part of the city as the minster.

Schascha decided to find Carl. In preparation, she studied the appropriate specialist literature: her detective novels. It rapidly became clear that the Three Investigators and the Famous Five were all in complete agreement: she would have to sneak out to the scene of the mystery. From her books, she was delighted to learn that unguarded rear entrances were a common feature. Outside some, she might expect to find a huddle of dubious characters smoking, out of sight of their bosses.

Schascha put her detective ID, her detective watch with secret compartment, her around-the-corner periscope, her rapid-fire automatic detective pistol, and her invisible-ink pen into her schoolbag. Finally, the equipment would get the opportunity it had been waiting for!

After school the following day, she ran to the City Gate bookshop, which unfortunately had no rear entrance, and was equally decidedly lacking in dubious, smoking employees she could bribe and/or threaten with her detective pistol. In truth, Schascha wouldn't have had much to offer as a bribe, but it would certainly have been enough for a large Penguin ice cream at Pino's, which wasn't to be sniffed at!

She was forced to sneak in the front entrance.

Schascha pulled her cap with the fake pilot's goggles over her face, and pulled up the collar of her yellow winter coat to avoid being recognized. She sought out the most secluded corner of the bookshop, and pulled a book from the shelf to complete her disguise.

She had barely opened it before someone came up beside her.

"What are you doing in the erotic literature section?" laughed Leon.

"Eeek!" cried Schascha, dropping *Consuming Passion* on the book table, instinctively wiping her hands on her coat, and taking a few paces away from the book. Watching people kissing on TV was embarrassing enough.

"Are you looking for something specific?" was the question Leon should have asked. Unfortunately, he had no idea where anything specific could be found in the shop; the best he could have offered was a very nonspecific direction.

"Do you know Carl? The Book Walker?"

"He doesn't work here anymore. The boss kicked him out."

"What? Why?"

"Some guy complained—I mean, he was real loud, shouting and all—about Carl taking his daughter on his round. It hadn't been agreed, he was her father, stuff like that. But I can't think of anyone who'd take better care of a little kid than Carl. He's all right, that Carl."

Little kid? As if! This boy had no idea!

"I've got something of Carl's. He dropped it in the street. A key. But I don't know where to find him."

"I can give you his address—it's still pinned up in the office. Come with me."

Leon led her to the large windowless back room, where a page pinned to the wall contained the names, addresses, and phone numbers of all the shop's employees. Schascha wrote down Carl's contact details neatly in felt-tip pen on the back of her hand. Her first detective case, and a resounding success!

Suddenly, Sabine Gruber was standing behind her, smirking.

"Leon, what's this girl doing here? Isn't she a little young to be your girlfriend?"

"I'm nine!" retorted Schascha indignantly. "Close to ten, in fact. And girls are two years ahead of boys—sometimes even three." Schascha's tone of voice implied she definitely belonged to the latter group.

Not wanting to lose the temporary job Sabine Gruber had kindly offered him after his work experience, Leon replied meekly, "We know each other from school. She just dropped in."

"But what are you both doing back here? This room isn't for customers, you know that. What would people think of us if they saw this chaos?"

"She wants to come here for work experience," explained Leon. "So I'm showing her round and explaining everything. She doesn't think the mess here is so bad at all."

"That's right! My room is even messier... Sometimes, anyway...rarely, but it happens."

"I can't say that reassures me in a prospective work experience student. Now out, both of you." She turned to Schascha. "You're a little young for work experience. Do you even read?"

"Nope," said Schascha defiantly; she didn't want to talk to this woman about books and reading. That was something she could only do with people she liked. And this woman had fired Carl.

"Then we can't help you here, I'm afraid." Sabine stopped short. "What's that on your hand? Does that say Kollhoff? Show me!"

Damn! Why hadn't she used the invisible ink? The answer was, because it only became visible again when exposed to heat, and Schascha had feared the heat required would be too much.

Sabine Gruber reached out to grab her wrist, but Schascha darted away. For someone who had played hopscotch—and skipped endlessly around Carl—as much as she had, the slalom course around the tables and bookstands in the bookshop was child's play.

Not so for Sabine Gruber.

Once Schascha had escaped, she didn't stop running until she had covered the short distance to the address on her hand. She glanced repeatedly behind her, but no one was following her. Nonetheless, she wasted no time at Carl's apartment building, pressing his doorbell without hesitation—if indeed it was his. The name beside it was E. T. A. Kollhoff, but since there was no one else with that surname, she guessed it must be him. No voice spoke from the intercom; no door buzzer sounded. Schascha quickly pressed every single doorbell, and when a tinny voice asked who was there, she simply said, "Mail." That was what happened at her building.

A buzzer sounded, and she pushed the door open. She ran up the stairs, checking the names as she passed each apartment, to see whether Carl lived behind its door. Finding his name, she rang the bell three times quickly in succession.

Carl didn't open up.

He didn't want any mail delivered. All he received these days was final demands and advertising.

As Schascha continued to knock, he shut himself in the bathroom and turned the radio up loud. By the time she called his name, he couldn't hear her, not even when she began to cry.

Back at home, Schascha noticed her father's jacket hanging on the coat rack. It shouldn't have been there at that time of day.

She heard the sound of the TV from the living room. "Dad?"

Schascha hoped no one would answer. She held her breath, so as not to miss the slightest sound, and counted silently. *One, two, three, four, five, once I caught a fish alive…six, seven, eight, nine, ten, then I let it go again.* No response. Maybe he wasn't home after all.

"Hey, kiddo. Come in here, please."

Schascha stamped her foot furiously, then stepped apprehensively into the room.

All her books lay on the table. Her father had found them under the bed and carried them into the living room. The soft toy line of defense had failed to hold.

"Sit down, Charlotte. We need to talk."

"I didn't do anything wrong! I had to collect up the books, or the neighbors would've complained, especially Mrs. Kaczynski on the second floor. And I haven't been out with the Book Walker! Honest!"

"Sit down. Please."

"Aaargh, I haven't!" Schascha threw herself on the sofa in fury, pulling her knees up to her chest defensively. "Tell me the punishment first."

Her father frowned. "Punishment? I haven't thought about that yet. But I guess there should be one."

"Then think about it now. I want to know it straight away. Waiting for it is totally dumb."

"Do I sometimes do that?" His voice wasn't as forceful as usual. "Make you wait for it, I mean?"

"I don't know. Yes, sometimes. You're a grown-up, that's what they do. So tell me the punishment!"

He piled the books neatly on top of one another. "I don't know whether it's a punishment, exactly."

"How can anyone not know? I always know it straight away—punishments are always dumb."

Her father pushed the pile of books in Schascha's direction. Before speaking, he stared at her for a long time. "The punishment is, I have to let you stay the way you are. Wild and free."

Schascha sat up straight, leaning her head to one side. What was her father talking about? "Dad? What do you mean?"

"And I have to spend more time with you. Because I know you less than that old bookseller does." He sat down next to her. "You see, I..." He took a deep breath. "I was angry with him. With you. But actually, with myself. You won't understand that yet; I'll explain it to you when you're older." Schascha understood perfectly well, of course. But she was used to adults believing she couldn't grasp something. "I went and found him, your Carl, and talked to him—well, made accusations. I shouted at him." He bowed his head. "Truth is, I yelled at him, and I pushed him—hard. He lost his balance and fell."

Schascha was now standing on the sofa. "Did you help him up?"

"No, I...left him there."

"You're so horrible! You're a horrible man! I don't want you as my dad anymore!" She ran to her room and locked the door.

Schascha's father didn't force her to open the door. He sat on the floor outside and talked. In fact, he found that preferable: he didn't have to see the scorn in her eyes. She was his one and only: every day, the feeling gnawed at him that he was not good enough for her; not warmhearted enough; not attentive enough; not clever enough. Strongest of all was the feeling he wasn't spending enough time with her, and when he did, that he didn't make it meaningful enough. It felt as though she was taking a step away from him each day, that he was watching her get smaller and smaller, so small he could barely make out the details. Perhaps that was normal, but he wanted to sense the beat of her heart again.

So he'd read.

"You've often told me I should read books. That would be so great. But in the evenings I'm so tired, and a book looks like I'd have to put so much time into it. So I didn't even start reading. But your Carl, he tucked a book in my pocket. Said it was wonderful, exactly the right story for me. It was wrapped in...kiddie paper, with dinosaurs and flying lizards. What sort of a book for me would come in stuff like that? The only reason I didn't chuck it away on the spot was because I wanted to get away quickly. Didn't want anyone to think I'd pushed the old man over."

"But you had!" bellowed Schascha from her room.

"Yes, I had. But I didn't want anyone else to know that. When I got home, I unwrapped the book and shoved it in a drawer, just to get rid of it, so I didn't have to look at it anymore."

"Why didn't you read it? Carl knows which books help!"

"It was a kids' book. I've never read those, even when I was a kid." He rested a hand against the door panel. "But then I saw you'd collected up all the books I'd thrown out of the window. I had every right to do it, don't get me wrong: you lied to me—for weeks. Doing your homework, my foot! You were out walking with that bookseller. You still went out after I'd strictly forbidden it. But that's not what this is about. I saw how important your books are to you, and I felt bad that I'd thrown them away."

"So you should!"

He smiled wryly. "To get closer to you again, and to apologize somehow to you, I read your Carl's book. At first I only managed a few pages—I was just too wiped out in the evening by the time you'd brushed your teeth and gone to bed. But eventually I got into it. It's called *Ronia, the Robber's Daughter*, and it's about you, somehow. But it's also about a dumb dad, so it's not about me."

"Is too!"

Schascha's father had understood it as a story about a young girl who needed to go her own way, but who still needed her father, the robber chief. Of course, it was also about a boy called Birk, who was in love with the girl. Simon would have understood that part; he'd have been entirely indifferent to Ronia's father, Mattis.

"You can go back to your Book Walker," said Schascha's father. "But only if you and I do something together too. It doesn't matter what—you choose. But not reading—that's a step too far. What do you say?"

Schascha said nothing. Was this the right moment to tell her father the truth about what she'd done today? He couldn't get in anyhow—the door was locked. Alternatively, she could make use of the situation to get a raise in her allowance.

But Carl was more important. Much, much more important.

"You've just told me a stupid thing you did, and I was super nice, right? Understanding. Not holding a grudge."

"Why do you ask?"

"Yes or no?"

"Well, yes, but—"

"Good! Remember that!" Schascha stood up in her room and pushed herself up on tiptoe. "I haven't seen Carl on Münsterplatz for days. And last night, I had a really funny dream. Not funny as in laughing, I mean funny weird, and it scared me. I dreamed Carl was reading some books, and all the words he read disappeared. The pages turned completely blank and white. There's a special book he doesn't want to read, because then all the words in it will disappear forever. But someone forces him to read it, I don't know who, I knew it yesterday. Anyway, the words disappear again, but he disappears too, because the book is about him. So you see, I had to go look for him!"

"Is that why you're so late home from school today?"

"Carl's not working at the bookshop anymore, and it's your fault. The boss threw him out after you went there."

There was a long pause. "I'm...really sorry about that." He really was, although at the time, it had been exactly what he had wanted. Sometimes having your wishes come true can be a curse.

"You have to make it right! It's super important!"

"You think the manager will give him his job back, if I explain everything?"

"I'm super worried about Carl! I got his address at the bookshop. But he wouldn't open the door."

"Perhaps he wasn't at home? Maybe gone shopping or something?"

"I don't think so." She shook her head. "I can feel something's wrong, Dad. I'm scared something's happened. Will you help me?"

"On one condition."

"What? Don't say anything dumb!"

"On condition you come out of your room. We're going there right now."

Not even in the bathroom would Carl have missed the hammering at his door. Likewise his neighbors, poking their heads out of their apartment doors like cuckoos from a clock. Carl could hear them complaining loudly, and with increasing volume. He felt weaker with each chorus of invective. All he wanted was for the noise to finally stop. There was no alternative but to open up and take delivery of that registered mail.

"I'm coming!" he called, to put an end to the hammering. "Just give me a minute." Carl dressed neatly, and brushed his hair into place. There was no time to shave, but he looked presentable. If there was going to be a final demand pressed into his hand, then he'd at least be dressed correctly. He put on a false smile. It was one of Effi's—after all, she no longer needed it.

Holding the clothesline with one hand to maintain his balance, he opened the door with the other.

"You look terrible!" Schascha stepped forward anxiously, and gave his cheek a gentle stroke. "Are you ill?"

Carl saw her father and backed away. "Leave me alone."

"What's the matter with your leg? And have you got a stiff arm, or does it just look that way?" She reached out to touch his arm. Carl pulled it away, but couldn't hide the fact he could no longer extend it fully.

"Just go! I don't want to see anyone."

Schascha's father moistened his lips with the tip of his tongue. He wasn't skilled at what he had to do next. It had always been drummed into him that it was a weakness. "I'm... sorry I pushed you. Please accept my apologies. Is it my fault you're now—"

Carl slammed the door.

He no longer existed. And a person who no longer exists cannot speak with others. For days he had waited for one single soul to show they were interested in Carl Kollhoff, the person. Now Carl Kollhoff was no longer interested in other people.

That night, Schascha didn't sleep: she was busy hatching a plan. She'd packed away her detective gadgets: that was kids' stuff—this was serious! After Carl had slammed the door in their faces, she and her father had gone to all of Carl's customers to speak with them. The Book Walker needed to get back on the street, and it would take a whole city to achieve it.

Schascha wrote it out like a story—exactly the way it should all happen. She filled all the remaining blank pages in her friendship album. She crossed out and edited, marking places with a star where she made additions. It took hours. It all began with "Carl opened the door."

Carl opened the door. The intercom could take anyone's voice and make it sound like they were standing in an arctic snowstorm.

"Book delivery for Kollhoff," Schascha had said, "from the

City Gate bookshop." She had lowered her voice to a deep murmur, and added a cough for good measure.

Her throat was still sore as she arrived at Carl's apartment door. She was prepared for the door to open no more than a crack, and knew she would need to slip inside quickly.

Schascha laughed with glee as her plan succeeded. Carl hadn't heard a laugh for a long time, and a delightful laugh like this one for even longer.

"Hello, bookworm," she said, peeking into one of the rooms in curiosity. *"You've got no books!"* She ran into the next room, where there was an equal absence of books, just a bed frame, complete with rust, but no mattress. "Where are they all?"

Carl walked toward her, keeping one hand on the clothesline. "Where are they all?" He pointed to his head and his heart. "Here, and here."

"You know what I mean!"

"Sold. I don't want to talk about it."

It was clear to Schascha now that Carl was no longer himself: his face was too gaunt, his posture too stooped, the spark in his eyes too dim. He reminded her of a bloom in Mr. Darcy's floral clock, its calyx closed and bowed, waiting for the bright rays of the sun to fall on it.

That was her task. Today, she would be the sun!

"Ready?" she asked.

"Ready for what?" responded Carl.

"For your work, of course."

"Oh, Schascha, I don't work for the bookshop any longer. That chapter in my life is over. You could have saved yourself the trouble."

"No trouble. Now let's get down the stairs. You can lean on me—I've grown again this week."

"There's no point to all this. Leave me here."

"I want my favor," said Schascha. "Right now!" She grinned.

Carl gave her a long stare. "You've planned this very carefully, haven't you?"

"You had no chance!"

Arriving at the bottom of the stairs, Carl had to pause a moment for breath before they stepped out of the door.

"Part two," whispered Schascha, so quietly he couldn't hear it.

Her father stood next to a kind of walking frame with an adapted basket designed to transport books, even large-format atlases. He had also added larger tires and suspension springs to ease the journey over the city's old, cobbled streets.

"I chose the color myself," explained Schascha, "to make sure everyone can see you!"

It was a gaudy neon yellow. It probably glowed in the dark.

"Try it out," said her father. "I can adjust the size for you."

After a few adjustments, everything fitted, and Carl pushed his new vehicle for a few meters. "It may be a very practical thing, but the bookshop fired me."

"We know," said Schascha. "Everyone follow me. Part three! Hurry up." She couldn't wait for the adventure to continue. It was just as well Carl would be faster with the bookmobile than ever before. Before reaching Münsterplatz, they turned off into Frauenstrasse, not stopping until they reached the Moses antiquarian bookshop, where Doctor Faustus was waiting for them.

"Hello, Mr. Kollhoff, how exceptionally uplifting to see you!"

"Can you please tell me what is going on here? The others won't tell me a thing."

Doctor Faustus glanced at Schascha, who nodded. "Well then, at first, my efforts were not as resounding a success as your young companion undoubtedly imagined. Despite my most exceptionally eloquent arguments, Ms. Gruber declined to reemploy you. You can't reattach an old binding, were her words. The old binding gave me inspiration. Before I was acquainted with you and your service, from time to time I would acquire books from the Moses antiquarian bookshop. Their advice, at least, that of the business owner, was questionable, and several exceedingly mediocre works were recommended to me. In other words: they could make good use of you here. All further details will be explained by the business owner."

The door to the antiquarian bookshop had no bell; it squeaked.

Hans Witton was standing on a stepladder, dusting one of the old valve radios that sat atop every bookcase. He had once put his old radio in the window as part of the display, and his customers had promptly begun presenting him with their own treasures, on the assumption he collected them. He hadn't had the heart to refuse.

"Carl, there you are! What a to-do!" He climbed down and held out his hands. "I've been wanting to speak to you for a long time, but you always sent that young man with your books. I expected you to come in person. But all's well, you're here now. The professor has explained the situation to me, and kindly also drawn my attention to certain inaccurate historical works in my stock."

Carl activated the brake on his walking frame. "Hans, I honestly don't understand what I'm here for."

"Work, Carl, what else? You know as well as I do that since my wife died, I need someone like you here. You're familiar with so many books, and you can help people in their search. I'm good for arranging and dusting, and bookkeeping at a pinch, but since Maria died, I'm getting fewer customers all the time."

"That's very kind of you, but then I'd no longer be the Book Walker."

"You can be that in the evening."

"Who orders antiquarian books for home delivery? Surely they're the kind of thing people browse for?"

A sneeze sounded, and Mr. Darcy emerged from one of the aisles. "Excursion Day," he said, by way of excuse. "I don't know how the pollen grains find my nose among all the books here, but they are very successful. Andrea has recommended something to alleviate it, but unfortunately, the pollen remains undeterred." He walked over to Schascha, standing by her father and Doctor Faustus. "The young lady here had a good idea. One of many, it seems to me. I'm going to finance you, Carl."

"Finance? Finance what?" Carl looked around for help.

This is it, thought Schascha. Her plan would only work if Carl said yes right away. One little word, one huge impact.

"From now on, you'll be giving books to people who can't afford them." The words tumbled out of her. "They can contact the bookshop here, and then Mr....he will pay for them." She pointed to Christian von Hohenesch; she'd not yet revealed to him his true name. "Our nun is writing a press release about the project. She said she can do that, because she's had a lot of contact with newspapers over the past few years. And Mrs. Longstocking has promised to check it for grammatical mistakes. It's all sorted. You just have to say yes. Simple."

Carl felt old and frail. The feeling increased now that all eyes were turned expectantly on him, willing him to be strong enough to take on a new mission. "You've all put a lot of thought and effort into this, especially you, Schascha. But—"

"Here are the books that need to be delivered today," said Hans Witton, moving to a small stack. "They're for some very dear long-standing customers whose literary tastes I'm familiar with, but who have very little money to buy books."

"Mr. Witton can't deliver them," said Schascha with great certainty. "He has no time for that." She looked at the others: she had handed out good reasons written on slips of paper to each of them, for the purpose of convincing Carl.

"Besides, Mr. Witton's knowledge of the city is as deficient as his knowledge of books," added Doctor Faustus.

"The bookmobile doesn't fit him either. I can't adjust the height any further." That was from Schascha's father.

Doctor Faustus deciphered another slip of paper. "Additionally, Mr. Witton doesn't like strolling through the city in the dark."

"No one needs more reasons than that," said Mr. Darcy. "And now, you need to get these books delivered quickly. Otherwise...they'll wilt," he added, with a satisfied smile.

Carl looked into each expectant face. If all the world was indeed a stage, as Shakespeare once said, then it seemed the audience wanted an encore from him.

And no old trouper with any sense of decency could deny them that.

Slowly, Carl pushed his chariot toward the stack; he hadn't yet entirely got used to this mode of transport. Then he took the wrapping paper, scissors, and sticky tape he was offered, to wrap the books neatly. After taking the recipients' details from Hans Witton, he stepped outside. Everyone followed him. Along the way, they were joined by Effi, Hercules, the Reader, and Mrs. Longstocking.

Even Dog appeared, and ran around them, barking, like a shepherd's border collie. It had found its vocation.

"Has the cat moved in permanently with you?" Carl asked Doctor Faustus, who was walking beside him.

"Oh, it never stays more than a few days with me. It always comes back, but only for the delectable treats, I suspect."

"No," said Carl. "It only wants you to think that. It's a matter of pride for a cat that lives wild. Otherwise, what would the other street cats say?"

It felt good to be walking again. To feel the city under the soles of his feet, to hear it, to smell it. Carl missed the weight of books on his shoulders, the feel of it diminishing with each delivery, but it was also a pleasure to see them in the basket in front of him, in the blanket he had placed there to protect their corners.

For a while, he said nothing, then he leaned over to Schascha.

"You organized this well. When there are no lemons involved, you do a great job."

"You're so funny!" She laughed. "You gave my father *Ronia the Robber's Daughter*. That was a smart move."

"Well, actually it was for your Simon. We should take him a copy too."

"He's not *my* Simon!" She pouted. "But the day before yesterday, when I cried because I got a really bad grade in sports, he came over and shoved me. But in a really nice way."

"You see."

"You can take him the book. By yourself."

"All right. I'll walk alone, and you can walk alone beside me."

Carl had learned he could not openly contradict this little girl. If little girls wanted something, they wanted it with irresistible force, and he was much too old to be an immovable object.

"I've been giving your name some thought," said Carl.

"At last!"

"It wasn't easy."

"Course not, it's for me. I'm as odd as you, and I'm only nine. I'm bound to be even odder than you one day!"

Carl would have loved to stroke her head in reassurance, but he would have lost his balance. "At first, I thought you were like Bastian Balthazar Bux from *The Neverending Story*."

"But I'm a girl!" protested Schascha.

"Bastian has a vivid imagination, and immense power. But he doesn't realize it, so his name doesn't fit you. You know exactly how much power you have."

"Super lots!" Schascha flexed her little muscles.

"Then I thought I'd found you in *Ronia the Robber's Daughter*. But Ronia is a child of the forest, and you're a child of the city. You need your Penguin ice cream and lots of people around you. There simply isn't any book with a character like you."

"But you said you'd found one!"

"No, I said I'd thought about it."

Schascha kicked a stone.

"But the answer has just come to me."

"And you're only telling me this now?"

"I wanted to create some tension."

"You mean old man!" She grinned. "Are you going to tell me now, or do I have to start crying?"

"No, no more crying. I'll tell you: I'm going to write a book, like the Reader. And in it, there'll be a girl just like you, who I'll call Schascha. Then your literary name will be your real name."

"Will the book be about us?"

"Every good book is about real people."

"I meant, will Mr. Darcy and Effi, and the others, appear in it?" She paused, and bit her upper lip. "And my dad. My kind dad. Not the other one. He's gone now."

Carl nodded. "I'll write the book as if it's fiction, not a true-life story. Then Mr. Darcy, Effi, and the others will become what they have been all these years for me: characters in a novel. And even when the book is closed, they'll continue to live inside it. Schascha too."

"I think that's wonderful."

"Me too. Awesome, in fact."

As they approached the dark alley, Carl's pace slowed. It seemed gloomier than ever before. All at once, he felt a hand on his shoulder. It was trembling, and Carl turned to see who it belonged to. It was Schascha's father.

Other hands joined it.

Carl took a deep breath.

"You'll have to come with me every evening from now on, you know that, don't you?"

There was the sound of laughter, but it was the sound of joyful anticipation. It was part of Schascha's plan that from now on, an adult would walk with Carl every evening to be there for him.

Together, the Book Walkers trod the path through the darkness.

Because the books needed someone to show them the way.

★ ★ ★ ★ ★

"A book to snuggle up with, a book that warms and gives confidence. Just the thing for anyone who knows how important a good book can be."

—*Brigitte*

"At least as great as the story is the author's language: full of love, light-footed, powerful. You cry while reading, you laugh and sometimes you do both at the same time."

—*Freundin*

"Carsten Henn has written a sensitive, poetic novel about the magical power of books to connect people. This novel is a pleasure to read for all book lovers."

—*Aachener Zeitung*

"With this quite fabulous book, Carsten Henn provides a surprise. The Cologne native became known for 'culinary-vinophile' crime novels.... *The Door-to-Door Bookstore* is of a completely different calibre—one that turns out much more delicate and poetic."

—*Kölnische Rundschau*

"This is a feel-good book that caresses the soul and conveys the beautiful message of books that make you happy."

—*Ruhr Nachrichten*

Praise for *The Door-to-Door Bookstore*

"This charmer, translated from the German by Melody Shaw, is an unabashedly sentimental, determinedly uplifting novel about friendships forged through books."

—*NPR*

"Completely satisfying.... A specific kind of summer fun."

—*Los Angeles Times*

"The feel-good novel for all book lovers."

—*Spiegel* online

"The most warm-hearted and touching novel we could wish for as readers for this special year. It is a book that somehow hugs you when you read it, it really pulls you into its arms."

—*Deutschlandfunk*

"It is a warm-hearted story without kitsch with lovingly described protagonists. The right book for a dark rainy day, which immediately becomes a little brighter when you read it."

—*Westdeutsche Allgemeine Zeitung*

"The basic idea of the book—that an unselfconscious child turns the life of a lonely old man upside down—is not new. But Henn has created characters with great empathy who quickly grow on you."

—*Kölner Stadt-Anzeiger*

"Henn's novel is a declaration of love for the written word, a cheerful, fast-reading feel-good book for in between."

—*Westfalen-Blatt*

"A book that is about books must be written in an appropriate style. Carsten Henn succeeds in this with wonderful formulations and sentences that you want to learn by heart right away. A book to read often and again."

—*WDR 4 Hier und heute*